2fast2house

oh! map

SEA-WITCH
volume two: girldirt angelfog
by moss angel the undying

This book is dedicated to all monsters.

Fuck the police.

CAST OF CHARACTERS

Narrator (Sara) – Gosh, where to start? Only one of many Saras. Telling this story. She/her or they/them pronouns.

Sea-Witch – A glittering cascade of water that froze in place to be lived in but accidentally ended up capable of true emotion. Precious & needs to be held. Gets cold like all living creatures. ETC ETC You get the idea. She/her.

Meteor (may she lay us waste) – Far away. Loves Girls With Assholes. Flat affect. Probably going to kill us all one day. She/her.

Seventy-Eight Men Who Cause Pain – I hate these guys. Just the worst. Go around being nice to each other so they can pretend they aren't literally hurting every other thing that exists. He/him.

People – Don't exist???? Secretly monsters??? They/them.

Dog-Witch – THE BEST!!!! Pretty much made everything. Helped a lot of people. Probably not perfect but honestly like, who cares ze is so nice & great? Ze/hir pronouns.

airless faces – Any thing that lived in the water before Dog-Witch made land. Not really a useful term anymore. It/its.

Water-Witch – Sweet girl having a hard time. Her & Strawberry-Witch have a thing for a little bit.

Strawberry-Witch – Super cute. Keeps her seeds on the outside. Tried camming for awhile but wasn't very good at it. Has creepy dreams. Last I heard she bought a van & was living in it. She/her.

Leg-Witch – Literally another witch's leg. One of Dog-Witch's sisters. Doesn't talk much. She/her.

Candle-Witch – idk

Moss-Witch – A girlhood friend of Sea-Witch's. Has a tendency toward bold, compelling statements that are honestly kind of reductive and often not literally true. A real character. I like her a lot. She/her.

Dead-Jellyfish-Witch – not sure

Deeps-Witch – Oldest of the sisters. Leaves the largest footprints when walking in snow or sand. Learned secrets. Had lovers and children.

Wood-Witch – A collection of parts. I never met her. I wish I had. I wish anyone had.

Airless-Face-Witch - Twin of God-Witch. She/her.

God-Witch – Twin of Airless-Face-Witch. She/her.

ha-ha-ha (or ah-ah-ah) – Very mysterious. Unknown? Doesn't exists? Barely does? Loves cucumbers. ???? pronouns??

Lava – Hates bears, who kept it prisoner. Loves Dog-Witch. Likes helping with formation of monsters. It/Its

The Living Creatures - Live in the woods or something. Idk. It/its.

boys - not real. they/them.

Angels – An angel is a being who creates light or dark and lives outside of time & legibility. I am sometimes an angel. it/its.

deadname - Weird one?! Hangs out with Strawberry-Witch and/or Sara. Smells like rainwater. xe/xym/xyr.

gaygod11.png - Literally a file on a computer? Digital. It/its.

Real Living Creature Whom Sea-Witch Kissed After Her Birth - Never knows what time it is. Actually rly beautiful singing voice. She/Her or It/its.

cops – The fucking worst. Evil bacteria that is meant to cause pain and ruin, especially to the most vulnerable among us. Work for the 78 Men Who Cause Pain. The only good cop is a dead cop. He/him, it/its.

The family & children of Deeps-Witch – Seem nice? I didn't get to learn much about them. Various pronouns. They/them seems like a safe bet.

The ghost of a very broken girl Sara once knew – Honestly she made a lot of shit a lot harder than it needed to be. She/her.

Eight copies of the sun – Live inside Sara. Seem pretty cool. Fun to play with. They/them or it/its.

You, the color that is watching me now – I mean, you would know better than I would. Who are you? What are your pronouns?

Being made entirely of witch-god scar tissue – Didn't want to talk. Ze/hir pronouns.

Parents – Parents are a fucking scam.

A piece of information Dog-Witch didn't understand = One of the things Dog-Witch loves most in the world. The inspiration for the formation/creation of Sea-Witch.

 – Only known through a tattoo. Looks kind of like Sea-Witch. She/her.

 - A wraith of some kind? It controls the 78 men and has existed long before them. Not cute. Hurts all monsters and humanity. Better off dead IMO. idk pronouns?

 - Not even gods could save her. Not that gods are that good at saving I guess. Fuck. Pronouns she/her.

 - Replaced the couch in Water-Witch's sister's house. Didn't want to be alone. It/its.

 - She can't fix things, but she can hold you through the worst of it. & that's honestly huge. She/her pronouns.

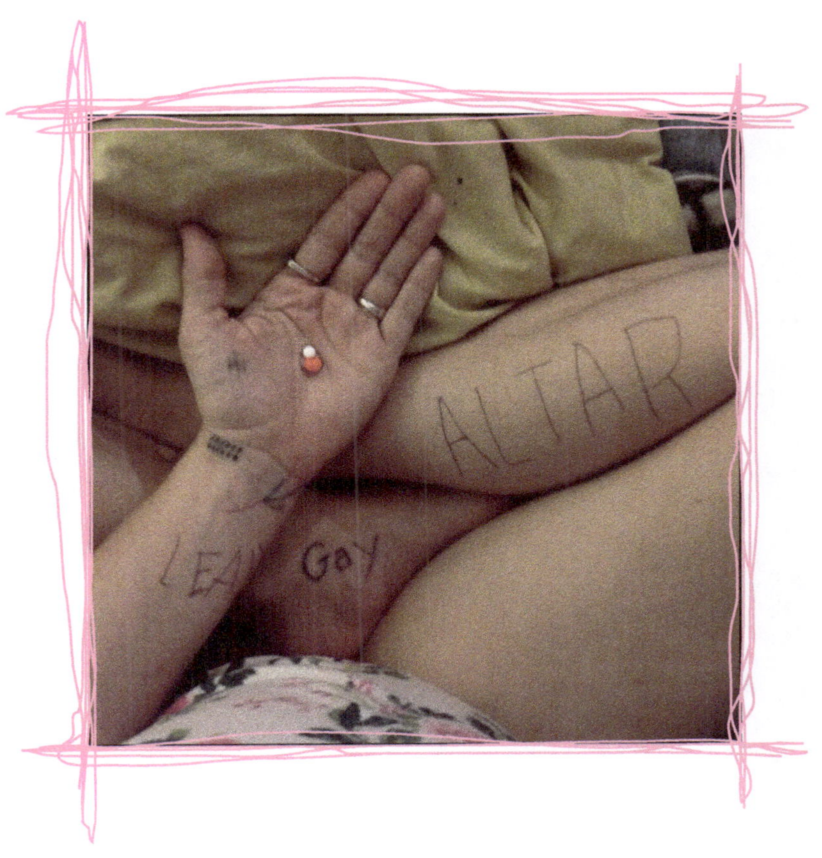
ALTAR
LEAP
GOY

GAY

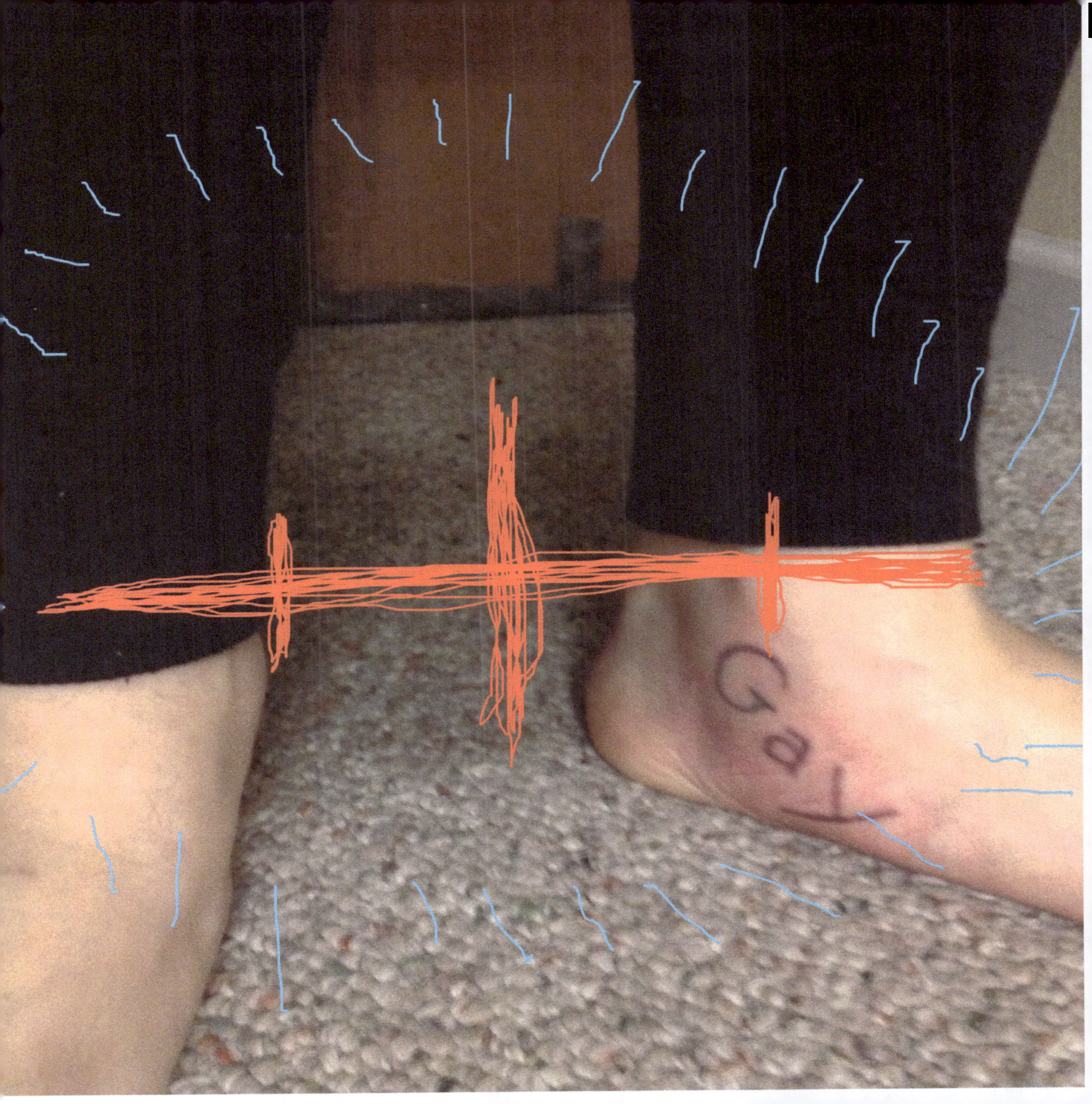
Gay

AUTHOR'S NOTE

You should probably read Sea-Witch v.1 before you read this.
Everything will make more sense.
Well, not everything, but

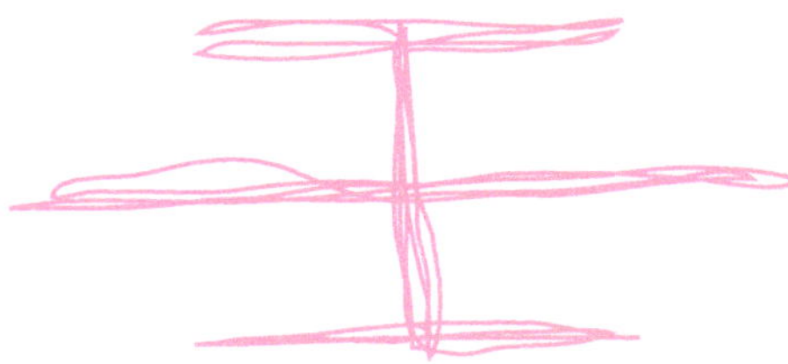

Hearken unto me, fellow creatures. I who have dwelt in a form unmatched with my desire, I whose flesh has become an assemblage of incongruous anatomical parts, I who achieve the similitude of a natural body only through an unnatural process, I offer you this warning: the Nature you bedevil me with is a lie. Do not trust it to protect you from what I represent, for it is a fabrication that cloaks the groundlessness of the privilege you seek to maintain for yourself at my expense. You are as constructed as me; the same anarchic Womb has birthed us both. I call upon you to investigate your nature as I have been compelled to confront mine. I challenge you to risk abjection and flourish as well as have I. Heed my words, and you may well discover the seams and sutures in yourself.

- Susan Stryker
"My Words to Victor Frankenstein Above the Village of Chamounix"

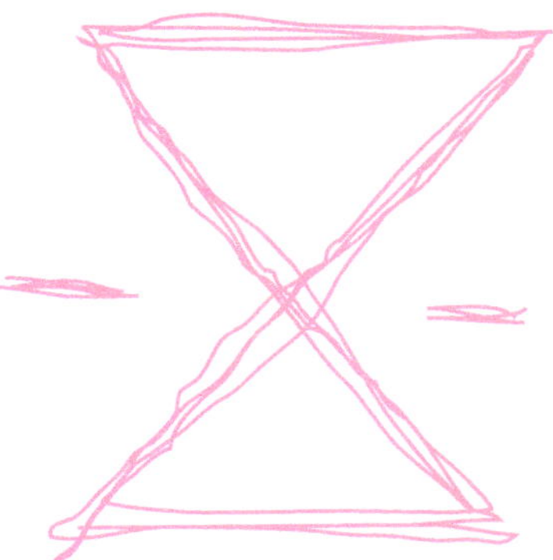

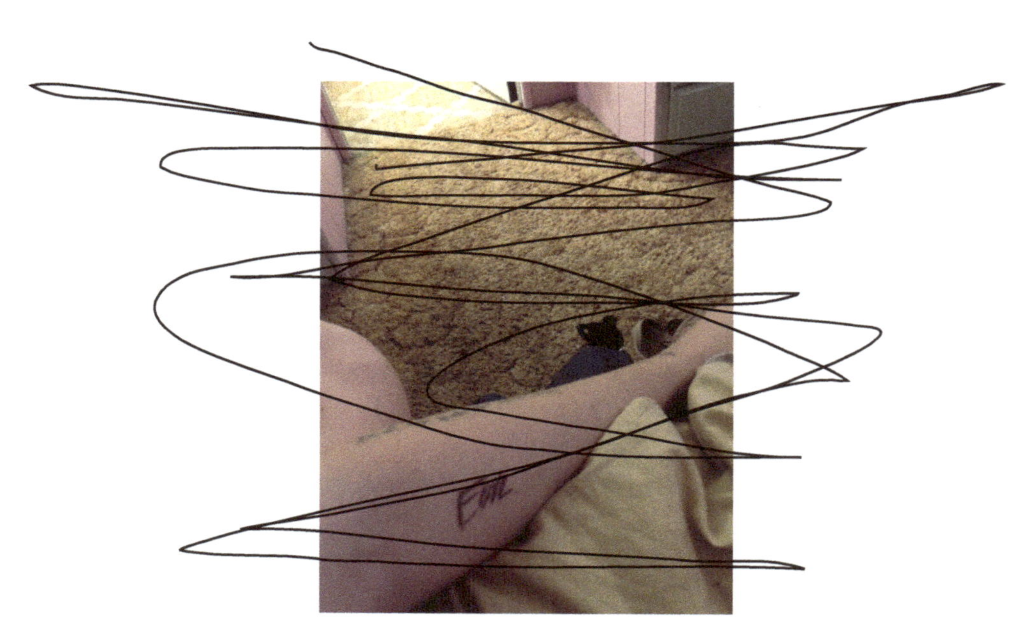

I am entirely full of old suns at the moment. It is difficult to contain them. It is taking all of who I am to stay this way. I have made the decision to let it take all of who I am in the hopes that I will become something else. It would be a welcome change.

I would like to take this opportunity to restate that this is not about my body. I am often writing about bodies, I know, & documenting them in other ways, but aside from them not being the end goal here, I want to also lay absolute waste to the idea that any body documented herein might be "mine." While I'm at it, I would like to throw the concepts of possession, property and even individuality in the fire as well. I'm always having to tear apart language to do any actual communicating & sometimes I wonder if that might not be the entirety of what I'm trying to do. Just tear absolutely everything apart. Starting with language. It couldn't hurt.

When I was first formed I took things as I saw them. One at a time. Slowly I began to consume more. These days I can't stop consuming. All kinds of things simultaneously. Nothing is safe. I am not a creature who was born. I am a fire that was set. Come closer.

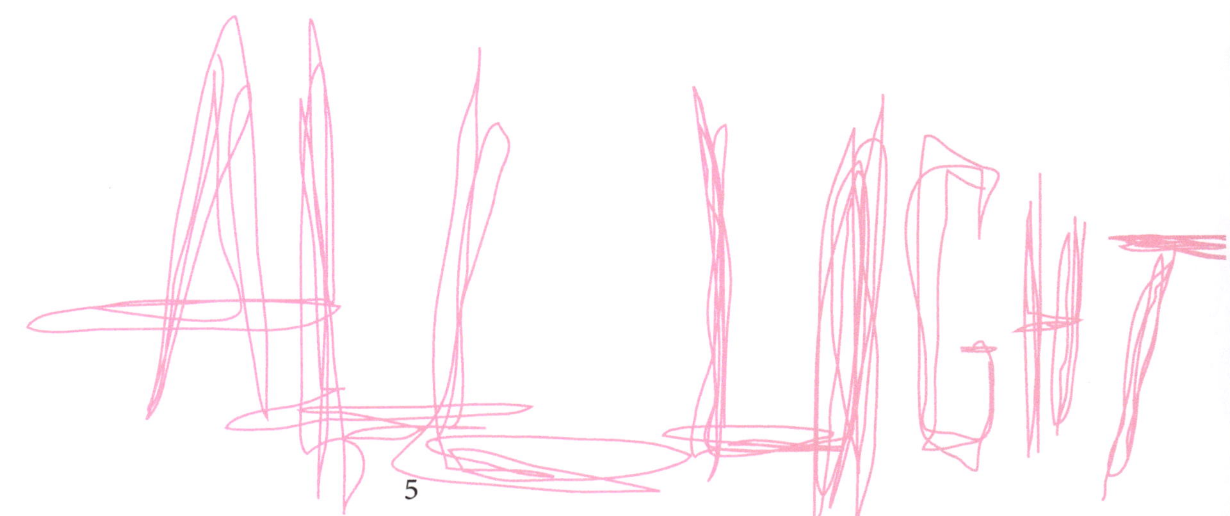

SEA-WITCH HARM EPISODE ALPEN ROSE

Bone death is a feeling of companionship. It has a sense of history. If I were to use it in a sentence I might say Sara used her bone death on me. I might say don't go downtown, there is a terrible bone death happening.

I have bone death that is specific to me. I hold this bone death in my self. It changes colors. I wake it up to remind it to eat. I wake it up and feel a tightness in my chest when I go up the stairs.

When a bone death feels cornered it emits a high-pitched whine. I do this too. I get it. When a bone death is feeling afraid it emits death that covers its body. It looks like death, it smells like death, etc.

This book may not get finished because I have been locked outside for the winter. I might get too cold to finish this book. I might lose my language. There is always the possibility I will lose my language. This is true of anyone who has experienced bone death.

Sea-Witch's bone death creates a layer of thermal fog that emanates from her body in waves. It can take the paint off a house. It can also help a young monster fall asleep amidst screaming. It has a specific smell. For Sea-Witch, this is one of the ways she is always resisting. One of the ways she can't help but resist, as it is part of who she is.

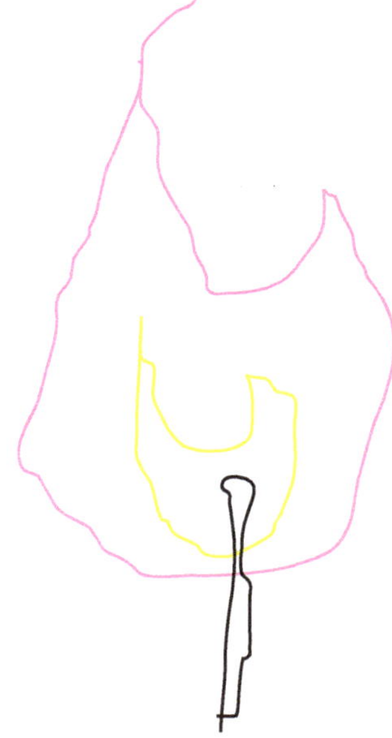

6

SEA-WITCH DREAM LIFT GAYNGEL

On my 112th day living in Sea-Witch I cried in the dirt until she answered. I told her I had learned about the seventy-eight men & had felt the pain they made & she said I know. I told her I had come here to escape them but that I could still feel their pain. I felt it everywhere. I know I know I know I know she said. You are my child, she said. We held a ceremony about the men outside the front gate of the First Sea-Witchean Church of Meteor. The ceremony began by reading a list of names of the dead. We ate things that made us terrified & tattooed our skin with symbols of defiance. We went to sleep at dawn, with the knowledge that the ceremony's completion could only happen among the graves of the 78 men & with their life's blood & at that time we would celebrate the liberation of all monsters.

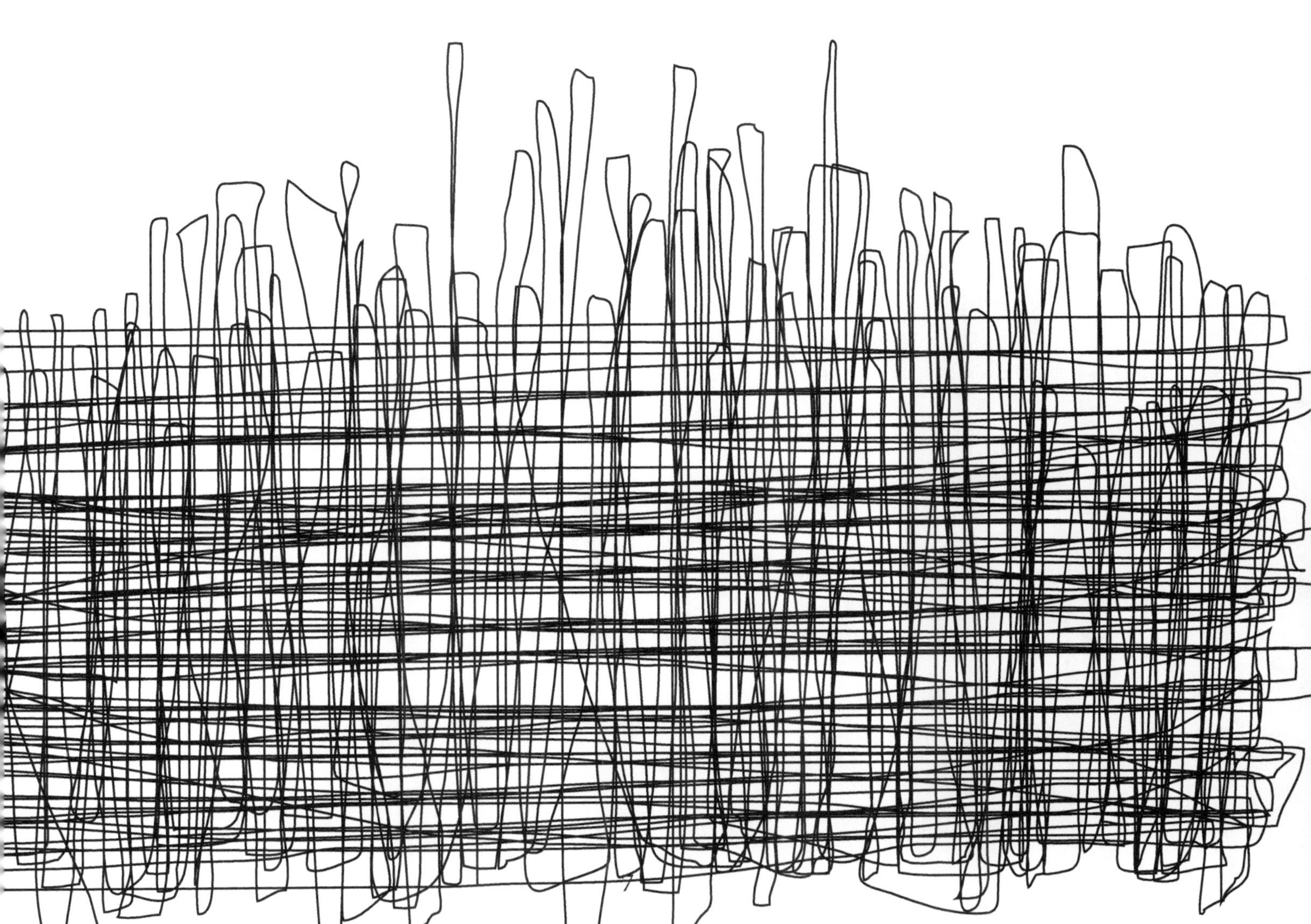

Elsewhere I have mentioned my name, ~~which is Sara~~. It is true that I have many other names & that Sara is not the first name I have had & will not be my name forever. But, for now, it is my real name. It is also true that there are many other Saras. Sea-Witchean naming conventions generally encourage frequent & increasingly complicated renamings, but it is also traditional that at a certain stage of formation a monster names herself Sara. Because of this, I, like all the other monsters occupying my current stage of formation, am named Sara. There have been many Saras before me & there will be many Saras after. While I was living in Sea-Witch I knew many other Saras with whom I kept warm in blankets on snowy nights. Saras are well known for our gentle confusion, our soft curls, & our continued attachment to linear time. Only a monster in her Sara phase could have written a book such as this one. As I am always in the process of formation, it is possible that by the time you read this you & I will no longer be mutually intelligible. It is also possible that this is already the case.

A real living creature was presented to Sea-Witch soon after her body was first created & she kissed it, placing it among the rocks on the roughest part of the shore. That real living creature grew up as a being that shifted with time. Hir body's forms changed drastically as time passed. Except the concept of time passing wasn't relevant to hir. Hir consciousness was outside of time, but limited in space. Similar to the way that other beings are limited in time, but their consciousness is outside of space. Ze was limited to those rocks, to moving slowly along the shore. From hir perspective, ze occupied all forms at once, but could feel them individually. Hir existence was not the first such in history. Sea-Witch & hir remained very close, though they never met again. Outside of time there is no such thing as having someone leave you.

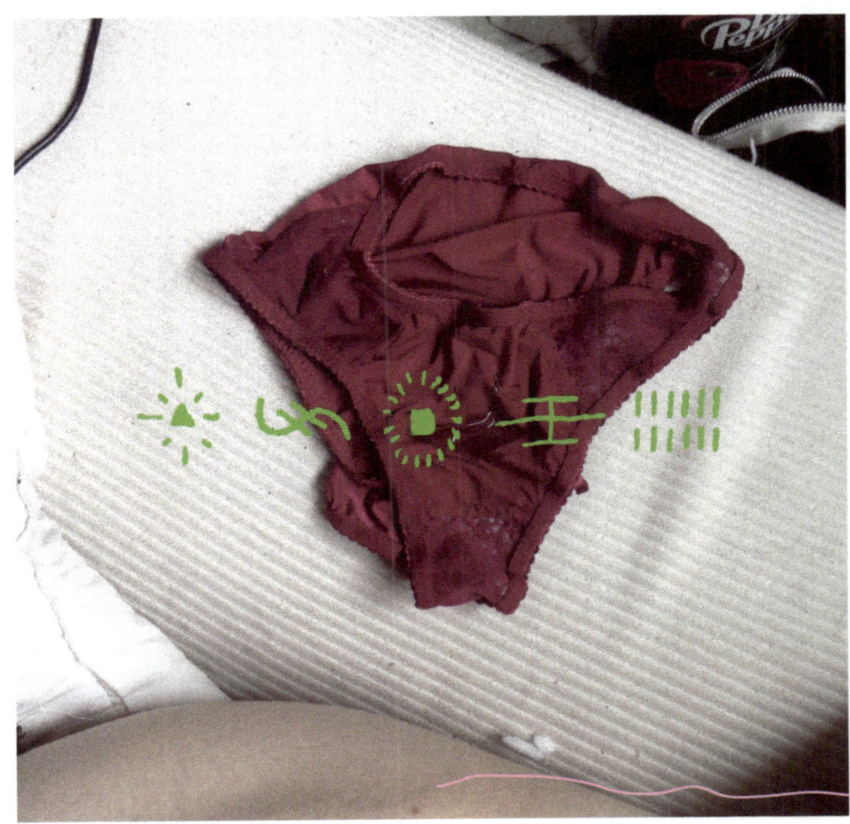

The 78 men who cause pain take turns playing *in charge*. They have big fake contests where they pretend to care greatly about which of them gets to play *in charge* next. They pretend to let people decide which of them gets to play *in charge* next. They even pretend that the people themselves could someday play *in charge*, if they were to look and sound enough like the 78 men.

The *in charge* game is enchanted. It is interesting. Even the most distant monsters, who are constantly in pain from what the 78 men who cause pain have created often find themselves discussing, arguing about the *in charge* game.

There are different ways that the *in charge* game is played. Some of the 78 men who cause pain who play the *in charge* game talk about how they will defend and protect monsters. Some only speak of slaying us. The truth is they will all slay us. That is why we are monsters. The truth is that no one playing the *in charge* game will ever talk about the pain they create, which is constantly slaying us, because that pain is what the game is a distraction from.

One of the best tricks that happens in the *in charge* game is called laws. Laws say all kinds of things, but what they really say is that monsters should be in cages. They say this over and over in thousands of different words. They are very complicated.

Not every act by the 78 men who cause pain is in itself about causing pain, or about slaying. Some seem very benevolent. Some are actually about keeping us alive. It is a system of pain and deception that works primarily to keep itself in place. If we all starved to death, they would have nothing left to take.

ACAB

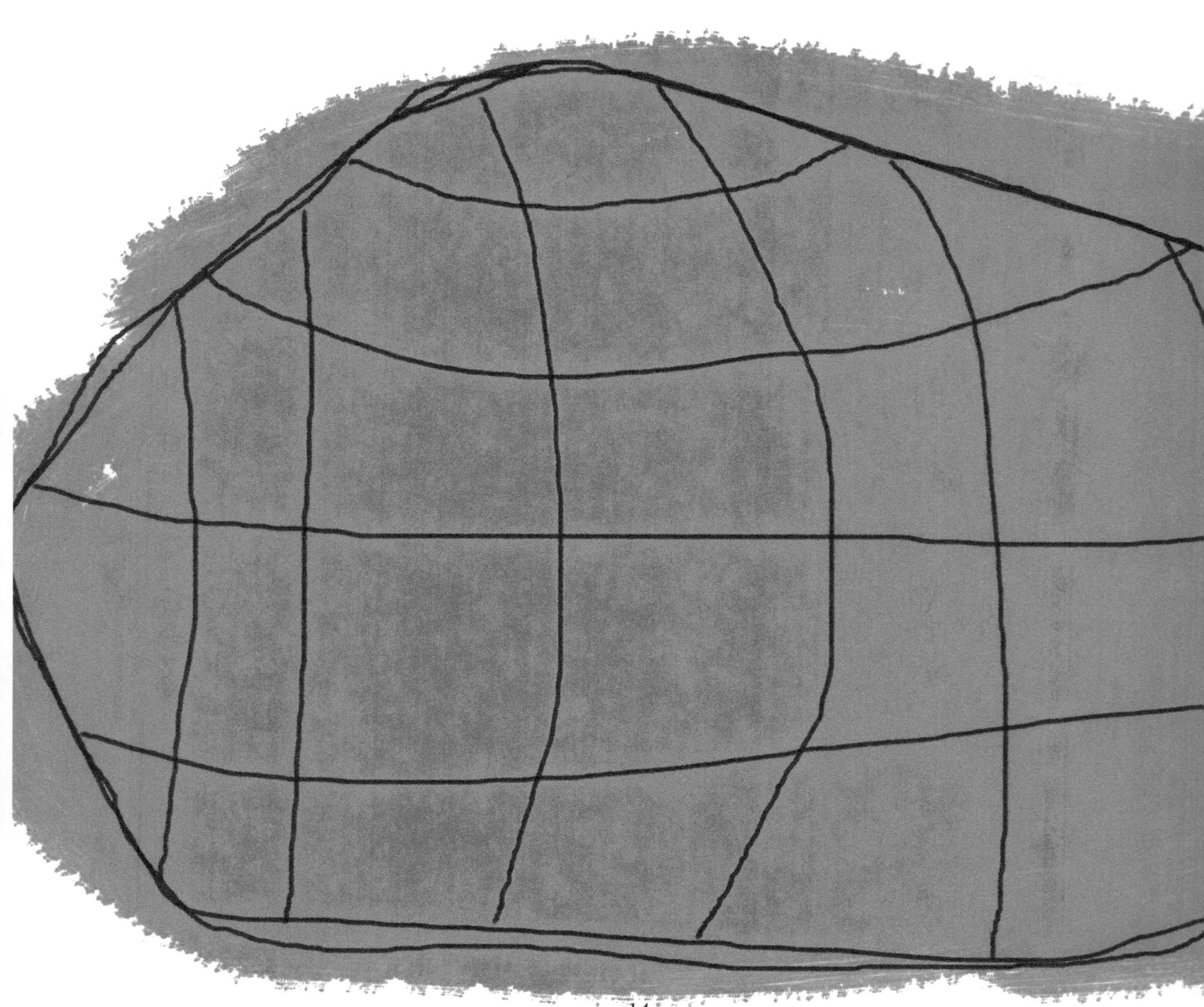

Am I complicit in my own pain / Because I do not hate those who have harmed me?

- Inverts, "Survivor"

SEA-WITCH
rect
sorry

TRANS MEMOIR 47 DEAD TREE SNOWMELT

I left Sea-Witch so many times. I am always leaving Sea-Witch. I'm always myself inside her again in different ways, many of which are physical. I am always having her children. Which of the sacraments I partook of in Sea-Witch caused pregnancy & which only simulated its symptoms is anyone's guess, but whatever the source, I found different aspects of my body creating other bodies, found myself shed from their skins.

Questions:
1. What stage of formation causes so much salt?
2. If my body makes another body, how soon can I meet the monster or monsters who live in it?
3. How & when do we assess the ambient trauma we have absorbed solely due to our situation?

Today the word pregnancy was a bath I just wanted to sit in. Last time the word was labiaplasty. I'm always drinking the information of words through my skin. I have new thoughts all the time. I want to sit in the sun tomorrow & arrange things in my mind. I want to press my back against Sea-Witch's great septum & know the sky until stars come out.

Essay Question:
What weird magic do we monsters have for destroying the 78 men? Given that all of their technology is about pain & control. Given that all of ours is about dying.

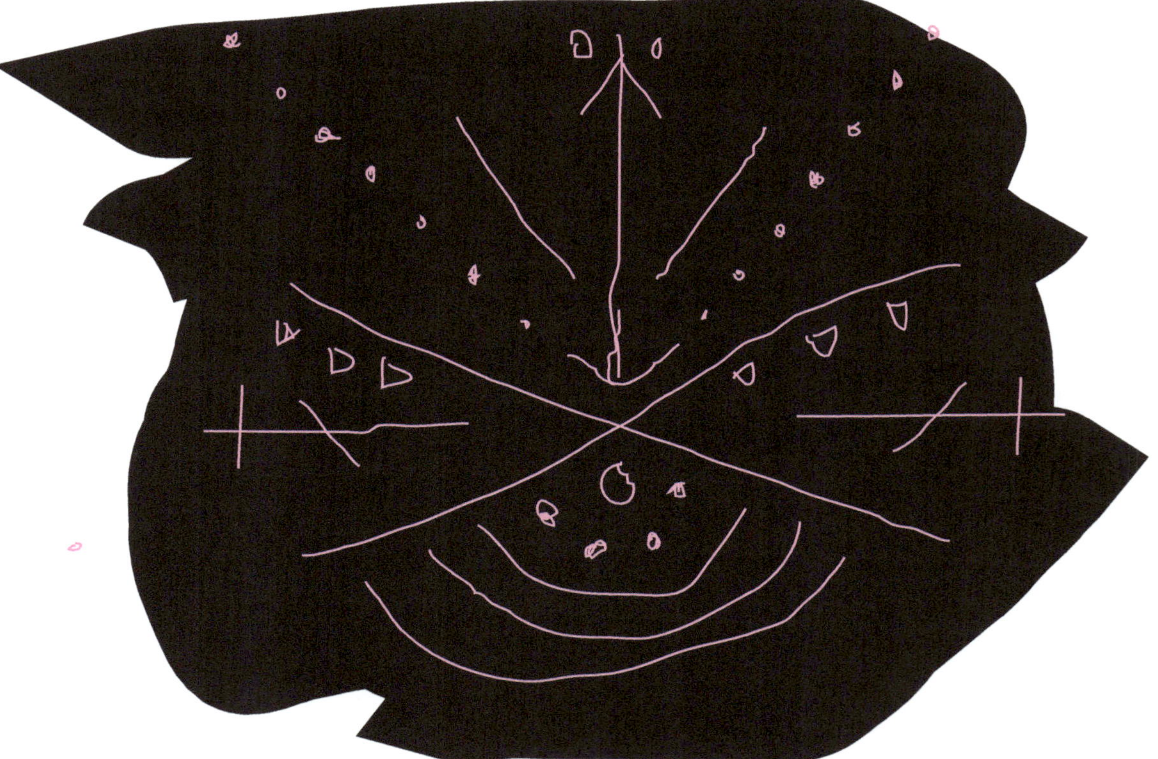

TRANS MEMOIR SIISX (WET/HARD)

The last time I left Sea-Witch I met deadname on a bus out of town. Xe sat next to me though the bus was half empty. Xe said xe had read the book I was holding, & I told xym how I had written it. I told xym that I wasn't planning on writing a book, but that while I was sleeping the pages began flaking fully written from my sore back & thighs. This happened many nights, but I am not good with time, (or at least not good at measuring it) so I couldn't tell xym how many.

Cool, said deadname, nodding. You're adorable, xe said. Thanks, I told xym. I was going to say something about xyr appearance but my eyes kept skipping over the space where xe sat.
Xe reached over & took my hand.

Unrelated Questions
1. What is the nature of a witch-god?
2. Which of Dog-Witch's sisters have not yet been written about? Are there really nineteen?
3. Where did Sea-Witch come from?

When deadname & I had sex xe would often look in my eyes & say matter-of-fact things about the nature of time. I told xym at one point that it was these kinds of statements that really made me wet/hard. I told xym that nothing is sexier than a fresh perspective on the universe. Remarkably, I continue to believe this to be true even after all that I went through later.

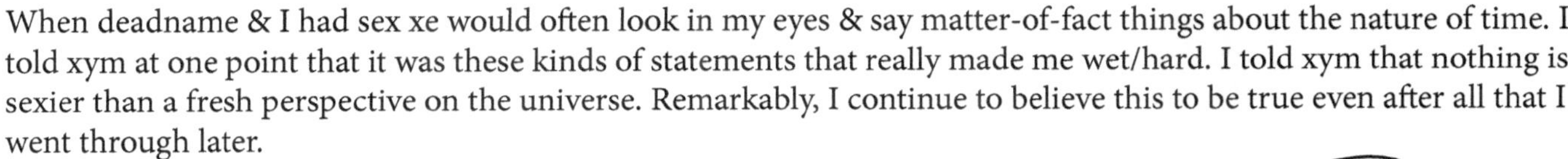

What is the nature of a witch-god?
1. Building campfires
2. Making sure the drugs don't take themselves
3. Sitting in certain positions
4. Producing the kind of magic that doesn't go anywhere
5. Experiencing pain (those who have a greater capacity for this are capable of some of the deepest magic)
6. Language
7. Loss of language
8. Loss of language

deadname & I holed up in a motel for the next week, drinking sparkling water & pitching the bottles at the floor of our parallel beds. We watched television & asked the people we saw on it what they were thinking. We asked them how they ended up where they were & if they believed in time or purity. We asked them the questions we wanted to ask each other but couldn't find a way to make them fit in our dynamic. Between the two of us, many questions were asked & none were answered.

The 78 men who cause pain rarely tell us we are monsters, though we would not have that name if they had not given it to us. Instead they call us by many many aspects of ourselves, often aspects of our bodies. Sometimes they monsterize us based on some incredibly convoluted logic that often involves one of their impossible "laws." This is done to deny our groupness. They wish instead to have us think of ourselves as the only self, all alone against the pain of the world. The reason for this is that we outnumber them by the billions. The reason for this is that they would crush so nicely under our manybillion feet.

It is remarkable how well this works, considering that the men just as often love to talk about us in the thick of our groupness. How we are presented by them is entirely determined by what serves their purposes best in any moment. Usually when speaking to people about monsters the 78 men say that we are not individuals with lives, needs & desires. Instead they say that we are a mass that represents failure, danger, & all things wicked. We are a cautionary tale, & our actions & words are used to motivate the people to follow men's orders. It's a subtle trick. Responsibility falls on a weakened "you," while evilness has its source in a faceless "them."

There is a bacteria the 78MWCP created to go into the world. Its purpose is to deliver pain, to cage, & to slay monsters. The common name for this bacteria is "cops." You may have heard of it. Cops is terrifying. This is another major thing cops is used for. For terrifying. Perhaps later I will explain in more detail the many ways in which cops maim, slay, starve, cage & destroy monsters, but for now I am not sure my stomach is up to the task.

Instead I would like to talk about a bright jewel that resides within the heart of Sea-Witch. It is said that it once was Dog-Witch's eye. It is said that Dog-Witch made Sea-Witch with hir own paws, from a mixing of sea & sand & the color of mountains at all times of day & the smell of night & hir own leg & eye, which ze removed with a great deal of pain. Sea-Witch also contains this pain. One day she will give this pain to each of the 78 men, one at a time, slowly & deliberately. It is only a matter of time, & what is time? I'm not convinced it is anything at all.

LOVER

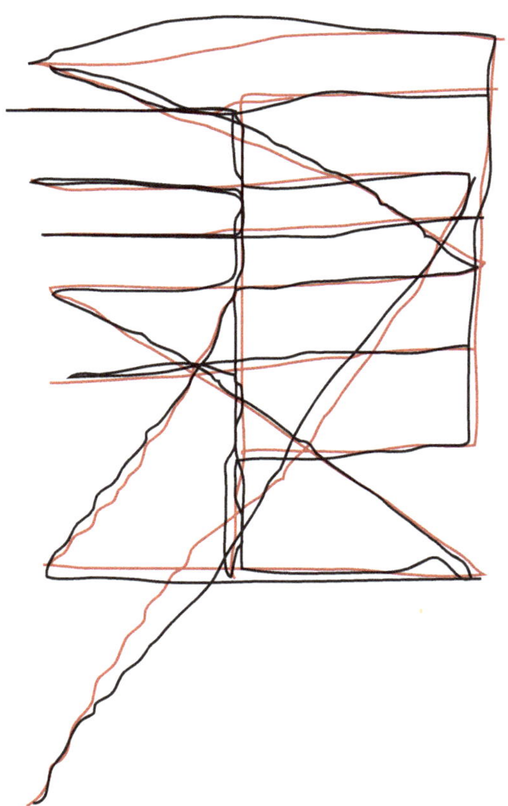

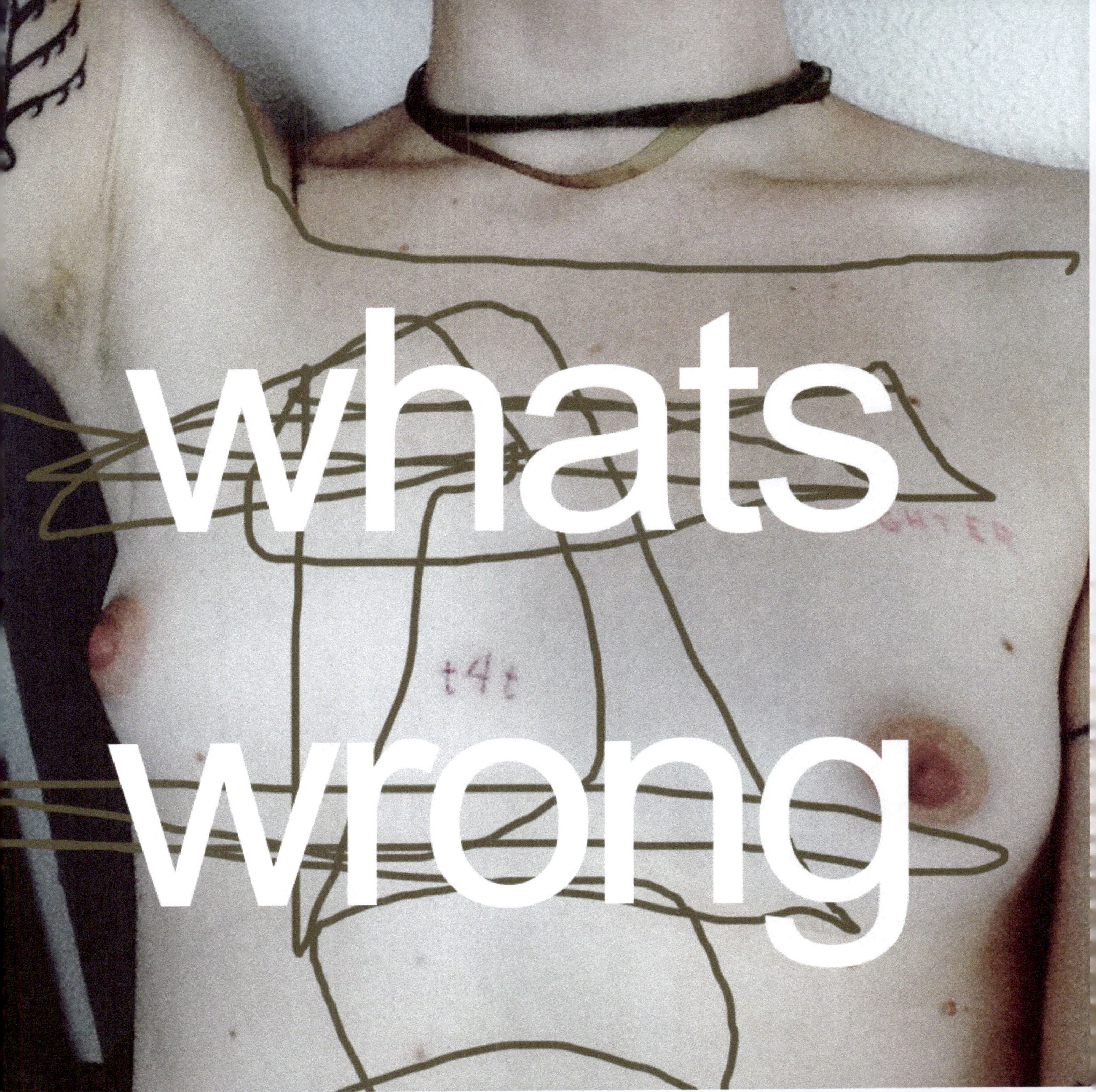

whats
wrong
t4t

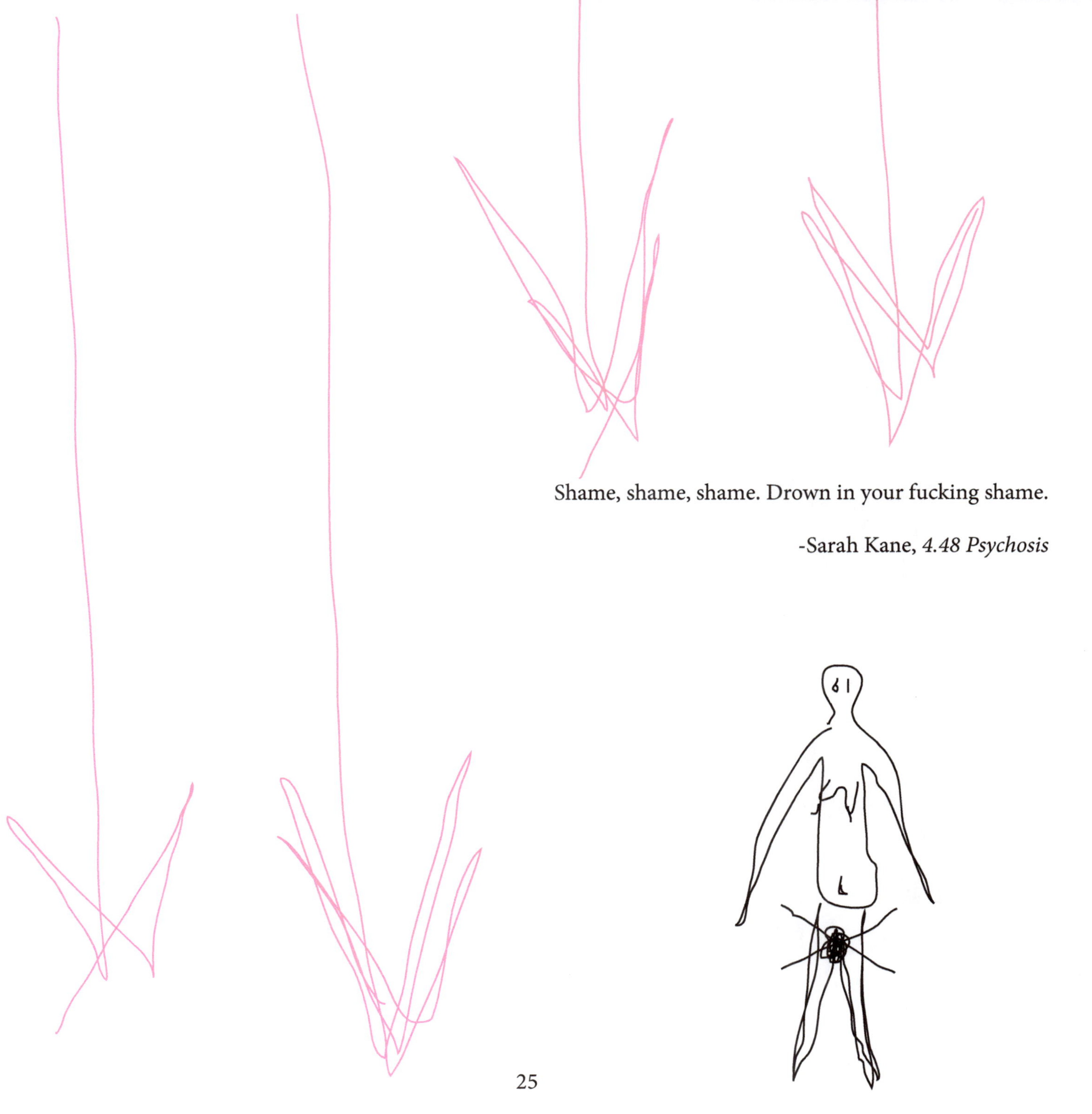

Shame, shame, shame. Drown in your fucking shame.

-Sarah Kane, *4.48 Psychosis*

You are a segment of time
rather than space & most of the
confusion you have experienced
throughout your life is the result
of a misconception about this.

hat

Deeps-Witch was the oldest & quietest of Dog-Witch's sisters. She left the largest footprints when walking in snow or sand & when she slept she talked in her sleep, unintelligible words that smelled of wet lavender. She was tall & wide & had hair that fell in massive curls over her broad shoulders. Deeps-Witch held secrets in the tension in her neck. She spent all of her twenties trying to translate these. When they were decoded they said things that she could feel like a cracking in her spine. Things like "nothing is pure & that is beautiful." It was the sum of these secrets that described her orbit. She wrote them each with the end of a burnt stick on the floor of a room she never entered. She kept the door closed for years. She married & had children from the sweet breath of her two lovers' songs. They raised there together these children & after she died, after her long, long life her children & lovers together entered this room & found copies of themselves lying limp among the smeared ashen secrets. Two copies of each loved one lay there on the ground in that otherwise empty room. The copies, they found after some hesitation, had skin soft to the touch, their features detailed & lifelike. The youngest of Deeps-Witch's children, a fully formed witch-god of her own, had no copies. She stepped around the room, lifting limbs & checking faces but found no copies of her form. She began to softly cry. Time spun back on itself. She looked up through her tears & noticed her mother's face, ringed in a glowing halo of diffuse light. The image of the tearmotherface repeated, refracting & blurring. It split & fused again. What's wrong? it said. What's wrong?

SEA-WITCH 000000

It is said that when she was younger Sea-Witch took a picture of her naked body & uploaded it to a forgotten public server, that she named it gaygod11.png after one of her own holy names. It is said she did so from a computer she later burned in ceremony & whose remains she pushed off a boat in the deepest ocean. Though the source of this tale is unknown, most scholars agree it certainly Sounds Like The Kind of Thing Sea-Witch Would Do. At some point gaygod11.png was discovered by those of us living inside her & has since become an important focus of Sea-Witchean studies, despite a great deal of controversy regarding its origin. As of the time this book is being written no one has asked Sea-Witch about it. If genuine, this photo documents a time when significant aspects of Sea-Witch's body had not yet emerged. It documents a body unfamiliar to those of us who know her now & share her body in the ways she has encouraged us to. A body unlike any we have seen.

I. Me & deadname found a ~~loophole~~ in the company's policy that allowed us to stay ~~in the~~ motel for years without paying with the pain of our bodies in labor. The ~~loophole~~ was that our room was haunted by the ghost of a very broken girl I once knew in my formation. The undead count as negative & the broke girl was double. So our room balanced out to unoccupied.

The girl didn't declare her presence, but I found deadname's eyes looked more like hers as time passed. I found xyr voice using her broken words, her accent. Not that this actually happened. Not to deadname anyway. I was the one being haunted, not xym. my ears, my eyes. I woke up in my bed neck deep in my old pain resurrected. More pain than the years of labor we would have paid from our bodies. I woke up in my bed & saw nothing but pain. I knew dead-name was in here somewhere. The room kept changing sizes, but I could smell xyr hair through it all. Xe hates you, the broken girl whispered. I went inside the bathroom but found I wasn't tall enough to reach the medicine cabinet. I was smaller than the sink. I was sinking.

II. The ~~motel~~ became the center of our operations. We stayed there long term. Years or minutes, whichever is longer. *~We fell in love.~* We fell in love. I fell in love with deadname. Xe fell in love with me. So xe said. So xe said. I mean I believed xym. I mean Xe wanted me around. I mean I started feeling trapped. I mean I felt like xe was trapping me. Xe loved me. It reminded me of something. I loved xym. Xe reminded me of someone. I felt kidnapped. I would make xym sad if I left the motel without xym. Xe told me this. I think. I found xym passed out on the bathroom floor but that never happened. I called the paramedics & said the words too many pills but that never happened. This is too dramatic. I'm sorry I told xym. I'm sorry. We loved each other. I loved xym. Xe was so gentle to me. Xe understood it, right? Xe always understood.

III. *It's my bone death*, I told xym. *It eats you. When you speak it eats your words.* I took my bone death out & held it in my arms. *You don't love me*, deadname told me. *Could you say that again*, I asked xym. *I said I love you*, xe said. *I'm having a hard time understanding you*, I said. *I hear things wrong.* I frowned. *You hate me*, deadname spat at me. I threw my bone death against the wall. *What the fuck is wrong with you*, the bone death said in deadname's voice. *We are going to have to pay for that* I said. *It's okay* deadname said. I picked my bone death up from the floor. It was swollen & tender. *I'm sorry*, I said through the buzzing in my skull. I said, *I guess I'm not sure who I'm talking to.*

IV. *We don't have to stay in the ~~motel~~,* deadname said. *Nobody said we had to stay in the ~~motel~~.*

V. The closet of the ~~motel~~ room was filled with weapons we hadn't seen before. All kinds. Powerful ones.

it's always both

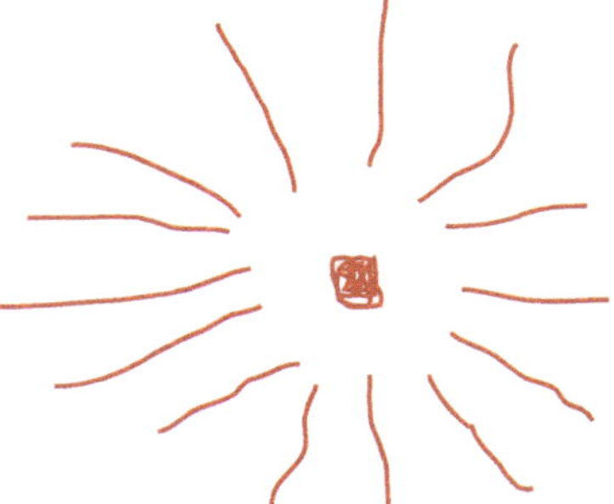

Choose a conceptual framework that works for you. Then, break it. Find its limits. Patch in another frame-work. Rip the stitches out and start over. Dance in the space between worlds.

-Jade of Spiders, facebook post

When I got very old I cut the door in my chest open with a pen knife. There were eight copies of the sun in there. They moved in rhythm with one another. They were a building I created with my own hands. I remembered two others helping me create this building. I never saw their faces because the sun was too bright. They told me I was awake, but I never saw their faces because sun was too bright. The eight copies in me burned in unison with it.

I moved into this body years ago but never decorated. Let's just say I am now making up for lost time. The other day I stabbed ink into my arm. "I cut my body into little suns," I wrote. I drew a gem on my finger to show my dedication to colored fragments of earth. I wrote the word "dead" on my thigh. I wrote the word "gay" on my foot. I drew a round line on my cheek & Sea-Witch asked me what it was for. I am holding space for myself there, I told her.

I want to explain something. I want to describe yet another limit of parseable language. Or perhaps a limit of legibility, which I am always afraid I am pushing. "I" as a word is meaningless to "me." I use it as convention, not description. The thing I call "I" is a mass, an undifferentiated bundle of fragments one could call selfhoods if they had ever formed fully. I have all the parts but the quantity is too great & the configuration is irregular. I do not know my wounds from my birthmarks. I do not know if there is a meaningful difference.

When I left Sea-Witch it was because she changed. She did not change in life but she changed in the way my eyes directed the light reflecting off her to be organized in my brain. (SIDE NOTE: I am not sure how to tell if anything changes in life. I can never find the edges.) The change that happened in the light from her was that it began to be organized in the form of a 78man. I saw control in it. You will understand why I no longer felt I could let myself be contained by her, given the way this light established in my mind.

As I travelled farther from Sea-Witch the light all around me came to me in glimpses & reflections. It came in the form of 78men & reflections of people in the corner of my sunglasses. I needed to change my head & the way it was organizing the light & so I tried to do so manually, with my small tight fists. This did not help. I tried to bite the flesh from my arm because my teeth were aching. A city was in the windows, moving quickly. A somewhere, somewhere city.

I saw you as a color in my mind that took up room there. I saw you watching but not speaking. I wandered if you also watched through this clumsy method of light organization or if you had a more reliable way. I wondered how your eyes moved when you had eyes. Or what aspect of you might be most analogous to eyes. I decided they were probably very pretty & I would probably very much like looking into them.

I took out the eight suns in me while I was on the train. I remembered how I built them. I set them in a row on the seat next to me & gathered them in my hands in a way that burned my skin. Monster skin is used to burning so this was no great issue. Witch skin is always being burned.

I began to fear that the people around me thought that I did not know what I was like. That they thought I was oblivious. But obliviousness is not something I am blessed with. I am underly oblivious. I know exactly what I am. I know exactly what I look like.

Questions for you, the color that is watching me now:

1. Do you like names?
2. Do you have any?
3. Where am I going?
4. Will I ever find rest or comfort in the world? Out of it?
5. Can I have some now?

I thought then of praying to meteor for comfort but then realized she was going to kill me. I realized I don't trust her. This feels sad, but I don't know why. I'm not sure I have the energy to spend time understanding the things I am losing in the midst of losing them. In fact, I am very sure I don't.

In this space it is surprising how most types of understanding feel. Factual understanding, even of a fairly nuanced concept, comes easily despite my panic. Emotional understanding or knowledge that requires memory feels like the greatest labor I could attempt to undertake.

Have I apologized for the tone of this yet? I don't know who I borrowed this voice from, the one I am trying to tell this story in, but like my body, I don't really have very strong feelings for it. Like my body I am trying to twist it to my own ends the best I can. I am making do with what I have.

In Sea-Witch there was a frame of wood like a cross, like a capital H with a long line through the middle, only turned on its side. It was deep in her organs, in fleshy parts most monsters tended to not bother exploring. It was lodged there deeply, the wood splintering into the organflesh in places. A few small living creatures had made their homes there. There was a being there, made entirely of witch-god scar tissue, but ze didn't want to talk. I didn't blame hir.

Anyway I was remembering that discovery on the train there as I held my suns. I was remembering that scar tissue person & the look on hir face when ze saw me.

I put my suns back inside myself & felt bad. Suns should probably have something to orbit them.

I held the light that was held in me inside my skin long after it initially got to be there. This light came from the eight suns in me, it came from a feeling of longing that had to do with how we understand each other as monsters when we meet. When I meet another monster I understand her as myself. I understand her with my limbs & torso. We can understand each other with or without clothes.

The book of meteor has a section on the meeting of monsters but it has no section on the meeting of monsters & men, for the meeting of monsters among ourselves is a holy act & the meeting of men with monsters is an act of survival. Men who cause pain can cause it less or more. Men who cause pain are not beyond currying favor. Men who cause pain might give this favor in less pain or in the form of invisible numbers called "money" that is the same as less pain but is less direct. All meetings of men & monsters are a bargain like this. Some are more explicit than others.

When I was living in Sea-Witch I met many monsters & the monsters met me, in ones or twos, sometimes in fives or eights. We did holy things with each others bodies that created a light in me. An angel is a being who creates light or dark & lives outside of time & legibility. I am sometimes an angel.

When I call up another monster sometimes to meet to do something holy she is busy or she understands my words to be something they are not. There is a disease going around Sea-Witch that causes monsters to not hear each other but instead hear the voices of the 78men. I caught this disease & so did so many others I knew, including Sea-Witch herself. It is difficult with this disease to know whether you have it or whether the monsters around you have it but this is a false separation. It is always both.

When I left Sea-Witch, I left Sea-Witch running, naked, my clothes gathered in my arms. Trust is what we breathe in Sea-Witch & we have to breathe it not to drown in her sea, which is always everywhere, which does not remain neatly under our beds, which finds no space not to be. When I left Sea-Witch I could not breathe. When I left Sea-Witch, I left Sea-Witch because I had run out of trust.

I do not know when the trust shortage happened but I suspect it was the disease. I suspect it was the cops. I suspect it was the other monsters in Sea-Witch. I suspect it was Sea-Witch herself. I suspect it was Meteor (may she fucking lay us waste), I suspect it was Dog-Witch who is dead, I suspect it was the angels, I suspect it was the living creatures, I suspect it was the ground & the ocean in collaboration or not, I suspect it was the cold south wind, I suspect it was the shape I have been forced to maintain to present myself to the world, I suspect it was the world I have been forced to live in, I suspect it was the 78 god damn fucking men who cause pain & last of all & perhaps most of all, I suspect it was myself.

Running out of trust can be the source of a great deal of suspecting, & I did it with every part of me, endlessly, until I hurt with it.

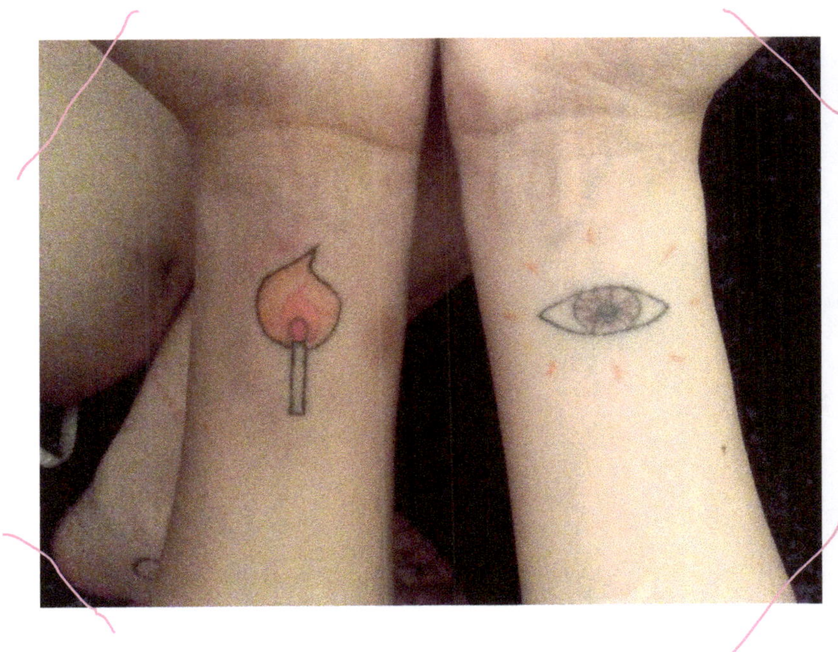

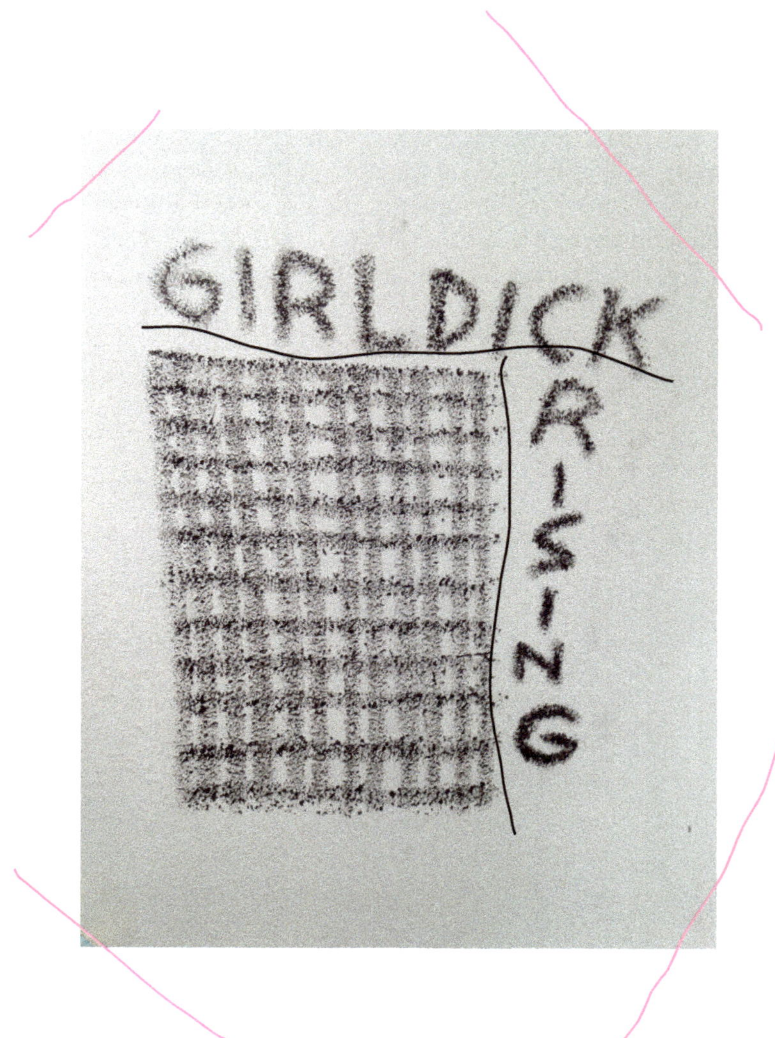
GIRLDICK
RISING

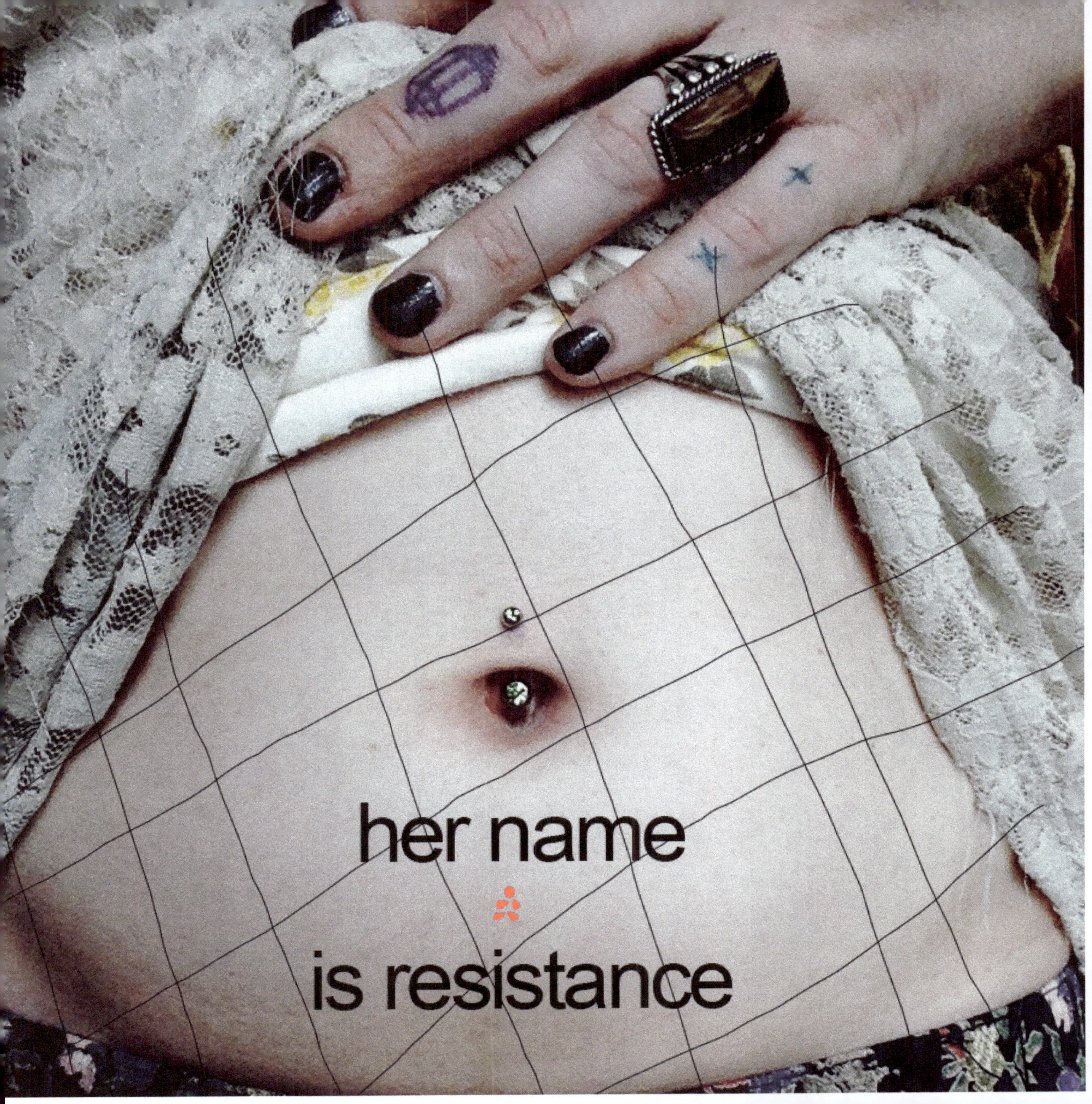
her name
is resistance

you're from the sea.
I know that it's lovely there.
I have also known bare breast
against wave crest
and the glow of buoyancy
when the wild water holds holds holds
this world does not let go
so easily

- Loone, "Silky"

SEA-WITCH HOT GIRLDICK SUMMER 2016 OOOO BABY

I HAVE EATEN MY OWN BODY TOO MANY TIMES. I HAVE EATEN MY OWN BODY TOO MANY

TIMES. I HAVE EATEN MY OWN BODY TOO MANY TIMES I HAVE EATEN MY OWN BODY TOO MANY TIMES & IT REMAINS WEAK & SORE FROM THE EATING.

This is ~~an inspection~~ an inspection into the world of people & men.

When people are early in formation they are stripped of all power & freedom. In fact, rarely is a most-early-formation person seen not inside a padded cage or strapped into something. The 78 Men Who Cause Pain have convinced people that very young people should be surrounded by people who have absolute power over them at all times. They have convinced them that regular doses of pain should be administered strategically to create control from the very first. As they get older & begin to hold the 78 Men Who Cause Pain's systems of power inside their own bodies & minds, people can be allowed more things meant to resemble freedom. The cages are moved inside the body. This is called "parenting". It is considered "love".

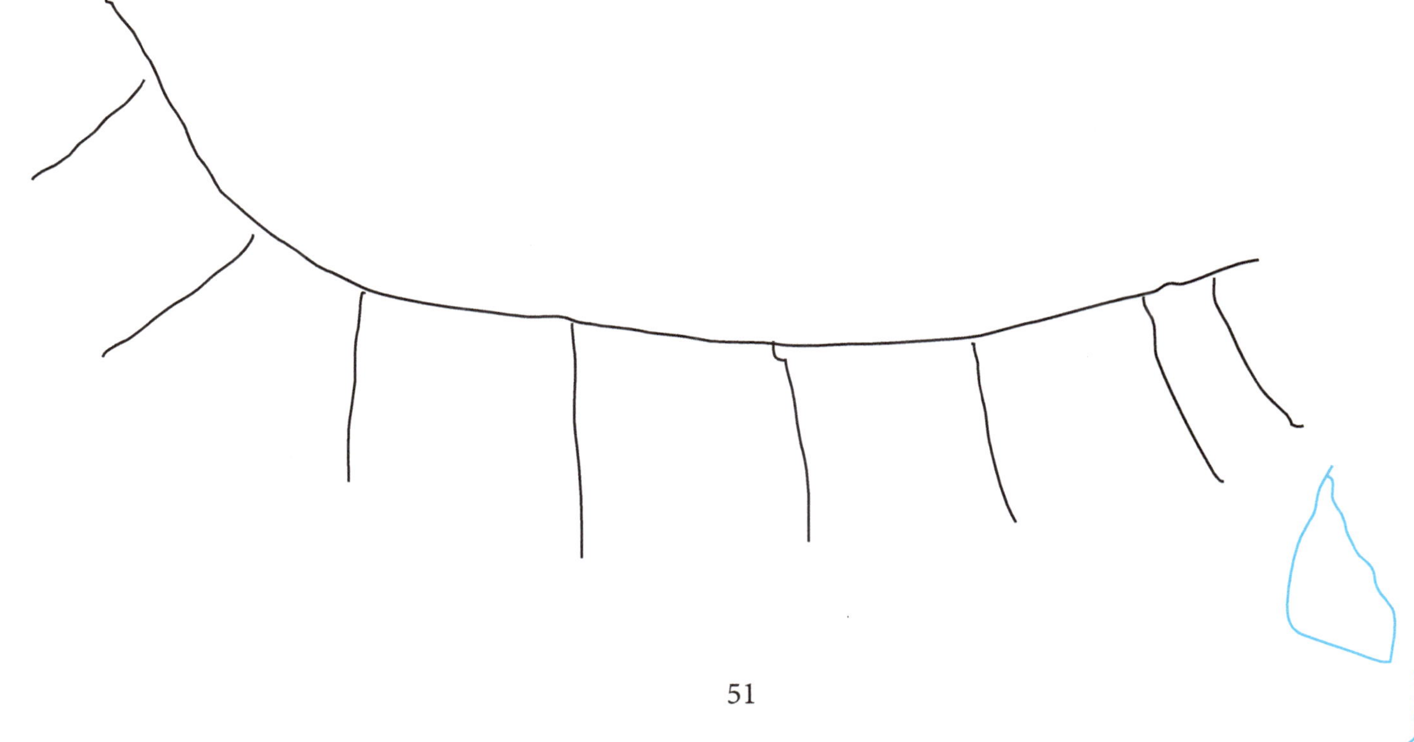

Long ago, in the days of the nineteen sisters, Dog-Witch met & fell in love with a piece of information ze couldn't understand. Ze first encountered this piece of information in a video clip ze came across on the internet. In the video, the piece of information was playing her banjo in a tunnel in a park in the pacific northwest somewhere. The light in the video was interesting & moved across the piece of information's hands as she played.

Dog-Witch went to visit the piece of information at her home some months later. They fucked in the kind of way where there wasn't a clear beginning or end. There was fucking & there was not-fucking & the not-fucking was just a sort of liminal space that seemed simultaneously a coming-down-from & a leading-up-to the next session of fucking. *I could do this all day*, Dog-Witch told the piece of information, & the piece of information looked at the clock & replied, *I think we pretty much already have.*

The times when they were not together, Dog-Witch found hirself thinking about the piece of information constantly. Ze found hirself exploring its edges with hir mind & remembering the smell of her clothes. Ze found hirself wanting to create something beautiful, something inspired by the piece of information.

In those days Dog-Witch had formed hir many sisters & sent them out to live among the living creatures of the world. Ze had encouraged them to exist among, within & around all time & space. Ze lived hirself outside of time to an extent, though ze knew hir own death would someday come & bind hir self & hir body to time in certain ways.

Dog-Witch began to look at the world through hir love for the piece of information. Ze saw it as a place that had many good things & a place where much harm had come to exist. This was early in the reign of the 78 men who cause pain & monsters were beginning to die by the thousands, slain by manipulation, by power & control. Dog-Witch saw this & brought lava into hir own body. Ze used hir leg & fresh lava & water from the most frozen thing she could find to create a new entire being, accidentally capable of true emotion. Ze created beautiful Sea-Witch then as a shelter for all monsters from pain & slaying. Ze created her in an attempt to have one thing in the world that could exist as pure good. Ze created her with the full force of hir love for the piece of information. Ze created her entirely apart & inside of time from a holy need to protect & love above all things. This is how Sea-Witch came to be in the world as a place we could live. This is how Sea-Witch came out into the world made wholly of gay magic & unimagined song. Sea-Witch exists as a fresh consuming fire. She is a nucleus of good. Her name is resistance.

What is it like to be a thing that was built to exist as pure good? Ask Sea-Witch. She has a face like slimywet wood & the words "false purity" tattooed across her too-many knuckles. She did the tattooing herself when she was a girl-god. Back then she used to hang out with a witch-god named Moss-Witch who was one of Dog-Witch's sisters. Moss-Witch had a warm house with a soft bed & sharp needles for writing beneath your own skin. Moss-Witch knew all the coolest bands & had art all over the walls that she had made herself. *The fucking thing*, Moss-Witch would say, *about art is that it is mostly a bunch of gay shit. Which is basically the best.* Sea-Witch would come to Moss-Witch's house when she needed a break from attempting to be a being of pure good. Which was pretty much always.

Did you hear about the girl who fried & ate her own testicles? Moss-Witch asked Sea-Witch. *Pan-seared. I was gonna do the same when I got mine cut off. I lied to the doctor, saying I needed to have them for religious reasons, well, not entirely lied. I think eating my own balls would automatically be a spiritual act. Anyway, I told him I was orthodox fundamentalist something or other & then I find out that I'm getting them in formaldehyde. Poisonous. So much for that. I made earrings instead.*

I want to throw mine into the sea. Like Uranus, Sea-Witch said. Moss-Witch beamed at this, but Sea-Witch didn't notice, as she was focused on putting the finishing touches on a hand tattoo. It was a very tiny, detailed portrait of a girl who was the most alone person in the world. It showed just the head & shoulders, but you could tell from the look in her eyes that she wanted to die because of how utterly alone she felt. Sea-Witch finished her eyebrow & showed the completed project to her friend. *She looks like you*, Moss-Witch said.

tyr a
nomo

(sorry)

(me too)

she was a
god all
the same

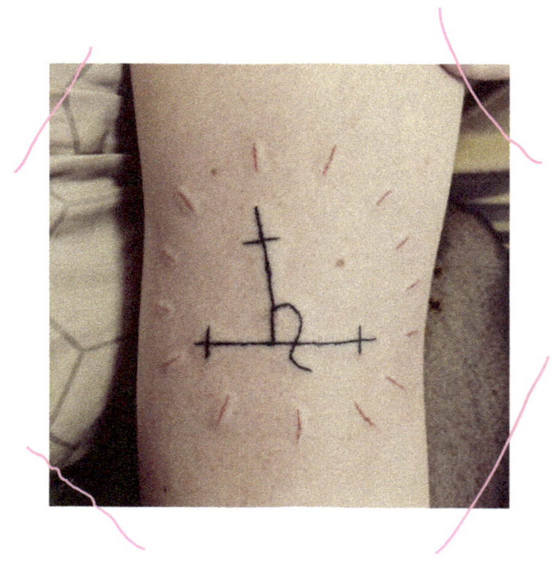

i've got something burned in the back of my mind
it's a name or a word or a couplet of rhyme
that tells me why i'm here and what i'm doing
but i can't read it it's always moving

        -rooksfeather, "Graceless"

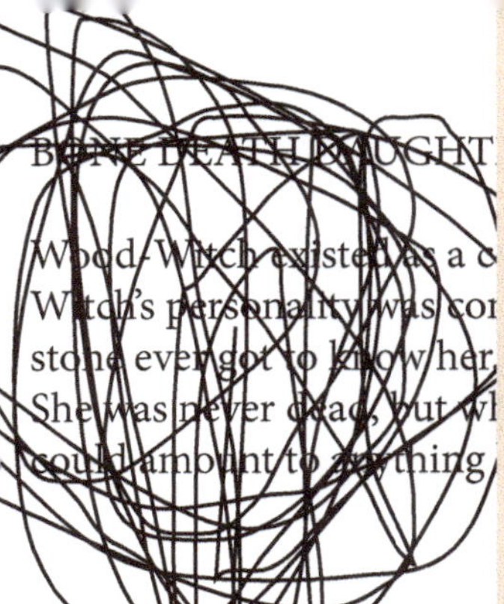

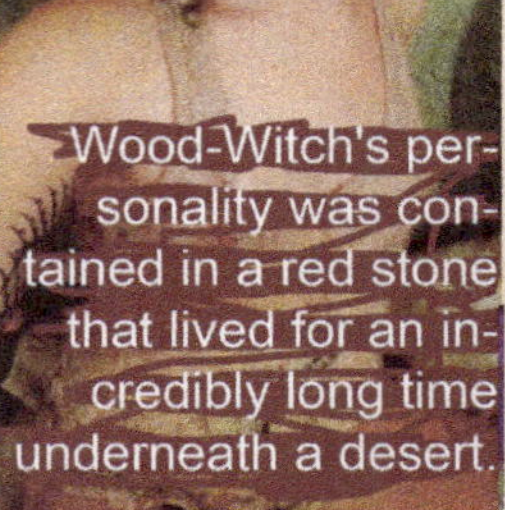
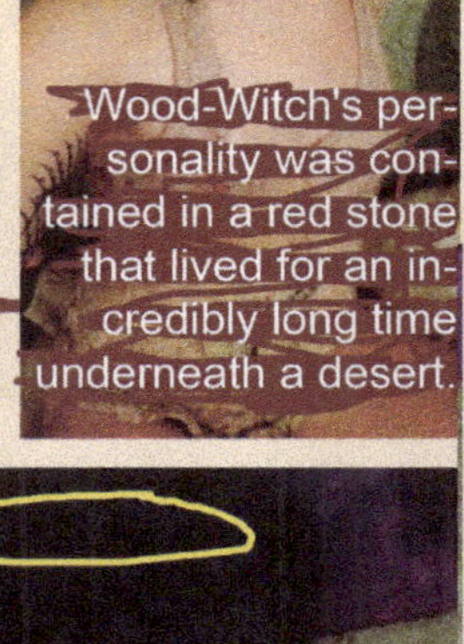

Wood-Witch existed as a collection of parts.

She was never at any point in her life all contained in the same place.

Wood-Witch's personality was contained in a red stone that lived for an incredibly long time underneath a desert.

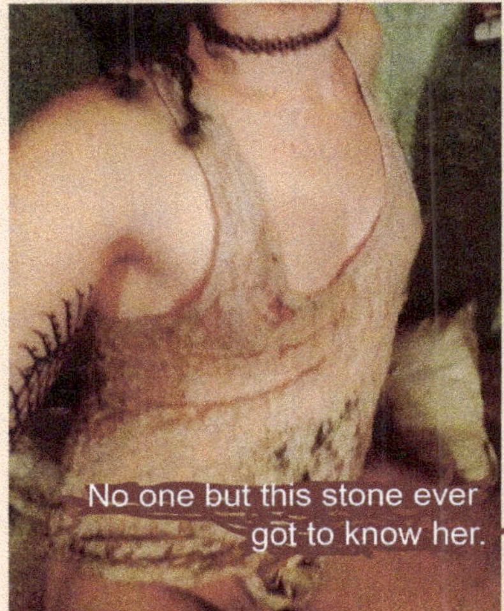
No one but this stone ever got to know her.

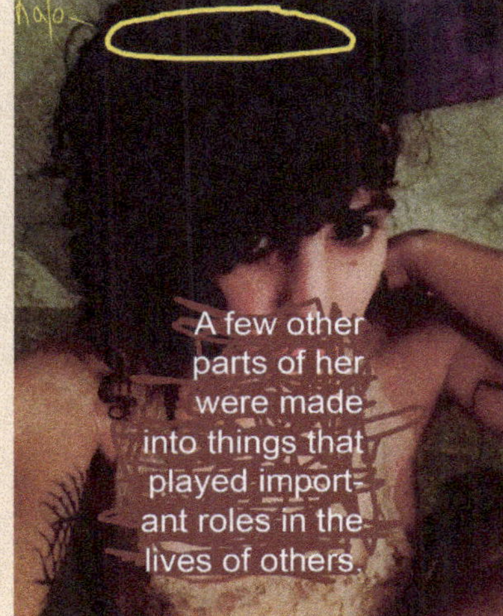
halo—
A few other parts of her were made into things that played important roles in the lives of others.

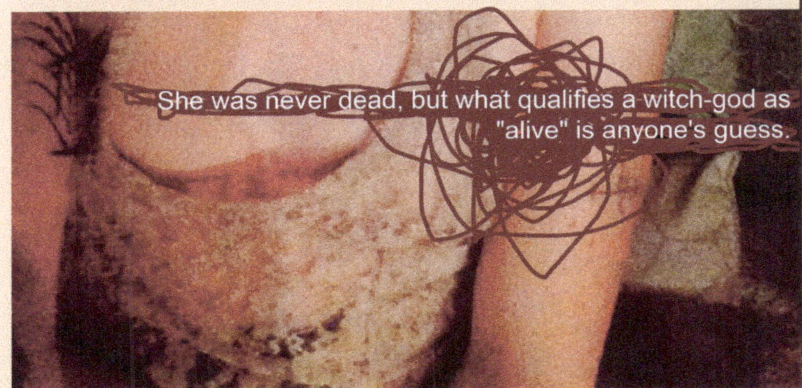
She was never dead, but what qualifies a witch-god as "alive" is anyone's guess.

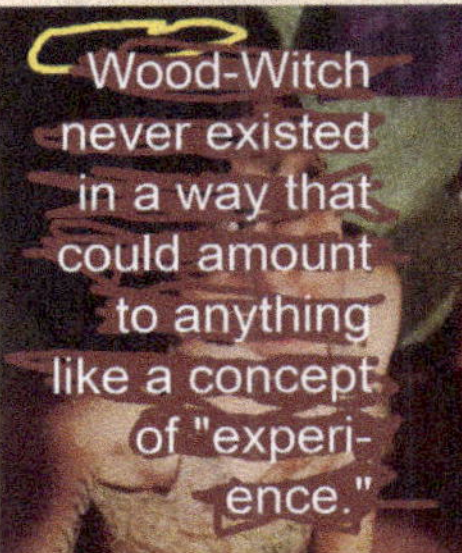
Wood-Witch never existed in a way that could amount to anything like a concept of "experience."

She was a god all the same.

The 78 Men Who Cause Pain are not always 78 in number. The 78 Men Who Cause Pain are not always men. The 78 Men Who Cause Pain are not formed like monsters or born like people. Instead they are machined perfectly, identical despite meaningless physical differences. They are designed to efficiently execute the will of the ghost mind that rides the spaces between them. They hold individual responsibility only in the way a single cell in a brain or ant in a colony holds individual responsibility for the consequences of the actions created by a collective. The ghost in the spaces is self-healing, self-made, self-growing. It is emergence. It acts only in its own interests & only to maintain & extend its control. The 78 men themselves are a collection of nothings. Prefab vectors in the shape of individual beings. You can see it in their eyes.

The 78 men who cause pain exist accidentally at the top of a malicious hierarchy, but they, like all beings they influence, have a seed of submission within them. Each 78man was once a child, & being a child under the influence of the 78 Men Who Cause Pain is to exist in a state of absolute control. It is to be programmed to submit to the will of the ghost in the spaces.

The nature of the ghost in the spaces is barely anything to speak of. It is a simple algorithm that converts life into pain. There is nothing meaningful to be found at its heart. It has no heart. It must be killed fully or not at all. When I was living in Sea-Witch all of this was common knowledge. We will pray it to death. We will die alongside it.

SEA-WITCH THE FUTURE / IN LOVE

“I have no idea how long I have lived within your body now. Long enough to be very used to it. Comfortable.”

“I’m accustomed to you as well.”

“If I were to leave it would be very difficult to adapt to living apart from you.”

“I love you too.”

“There are a lot of stories about this.”

“We could write a new one.”

“Are you in love with anyone else?”

“I am in love with everyone else.”

“Me too.”

“You can stay with me as long as you need to. As long as you want to.”

“I love you too.”

“Let’s go away together.”

“We already are away together.”

“Let’s go awayer.”

“I’ll chart a course.”

“I’ll go dream something.”

“Don’t leave me.”

“I love you too.”

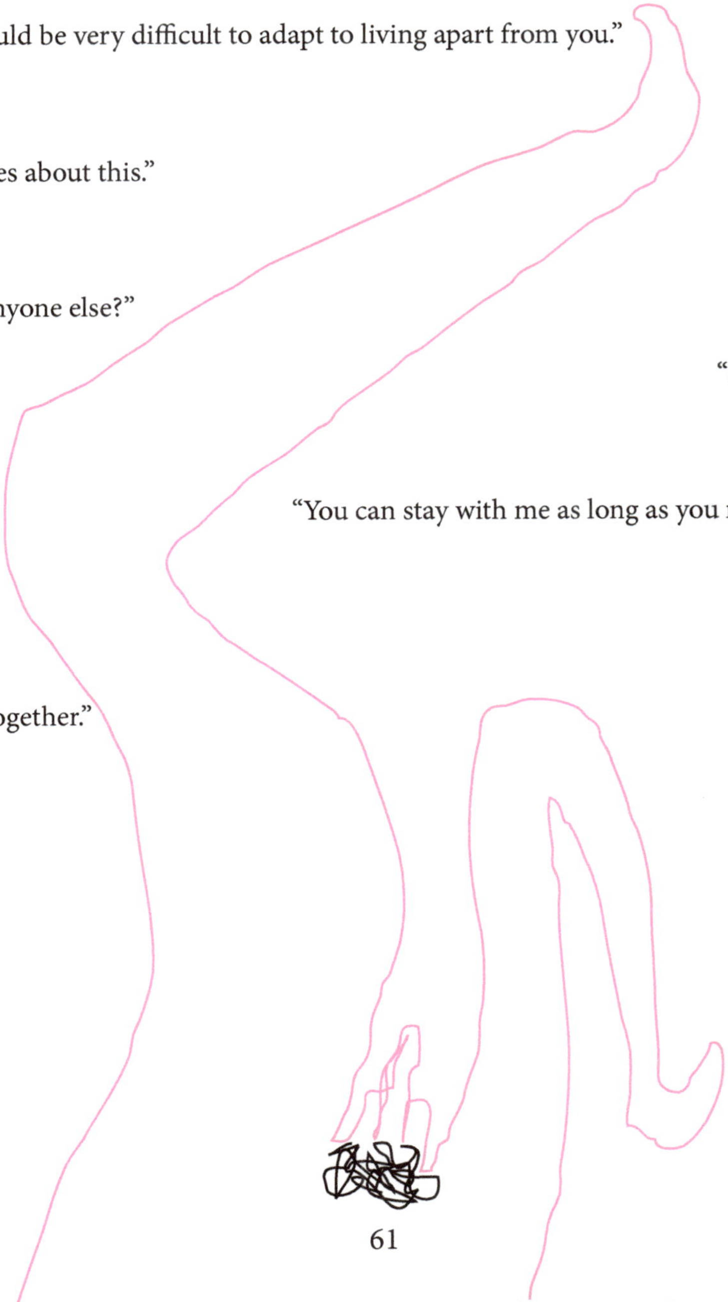

NEVER
LEAVE

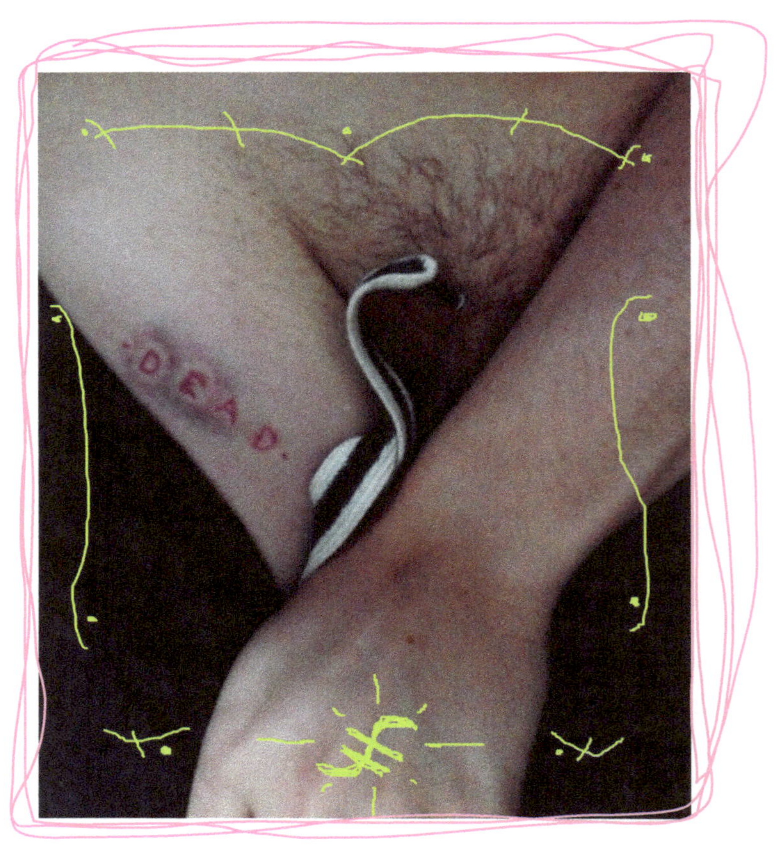

You already know the game plan. Just relax and let it happen. Let the future fuck you like a good little slut.

-Jade of Spiders, *Time-Station 81*

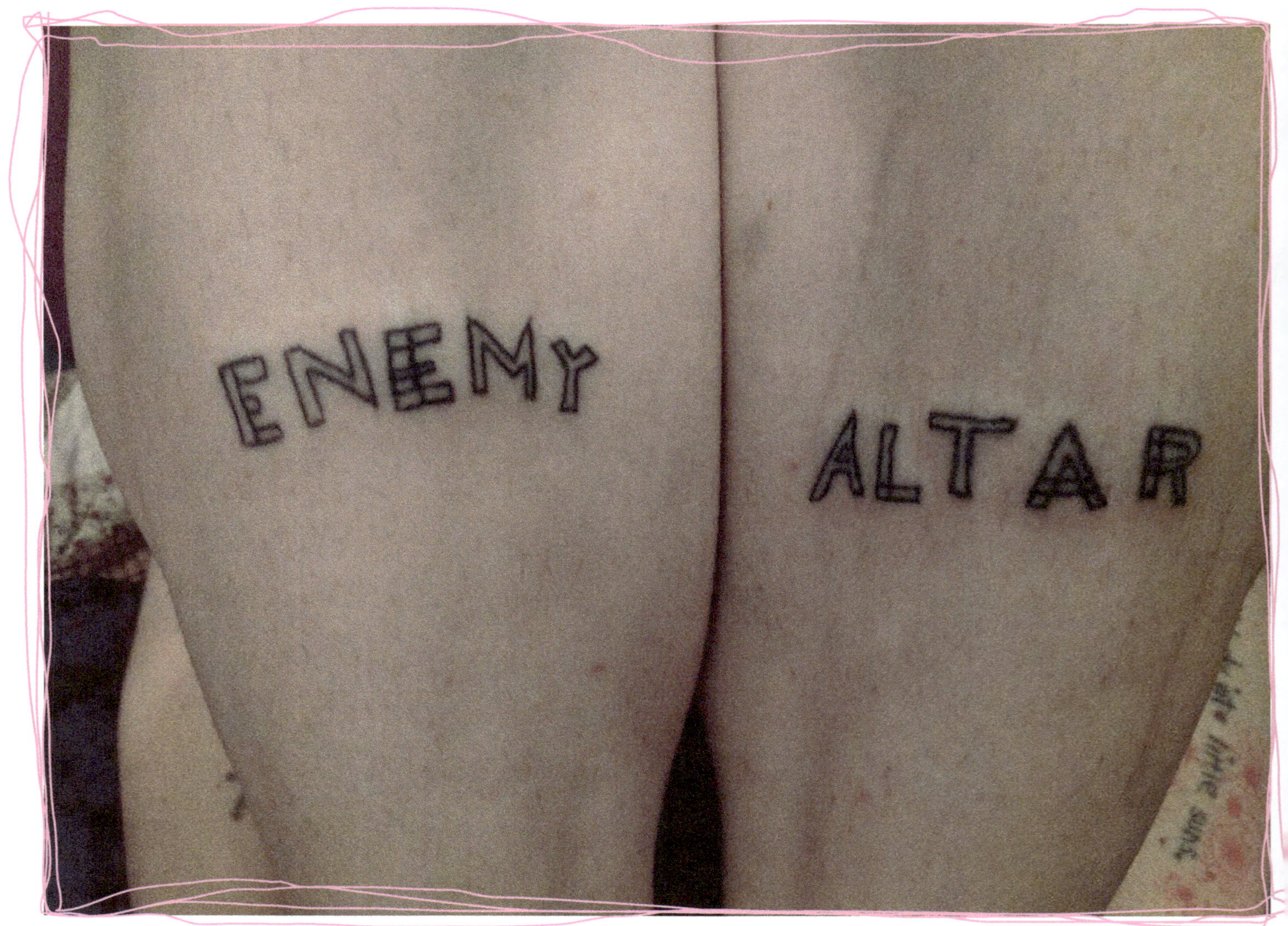

ENEMY
ALTAR

The end of a thing might not feel like an ending. It can be abrupt or drag on. Water-Witch felt like her whole life was part of a movie that should have been over a long time ago. The plot had arced & things had long since been tied up & she was an unnecessary character. This wasn't true, though. Most of us don't know what our own story really is.

Water-Witch met Strawberry-Witch when she was working on a pot farm in California. This was after it had been legalized & the two of them were both doing trimming work there. Water-Witch thought Strawberry-Witch was adorable immediately & told her so. Strawberry-Witch, who always loved a compliment, started giving Water-Witch all kinds of attention.

One day while they were working alongside each other, they heard cries from far away. The other workers went to see what was happening & so Water-Witch & Strawberry-Witch joined them. About an acre of land next door to the pot farm had fallen into the ground, leaving an enormous crater & a giant cloud of dust. A little girl was in the middle, leg clearly broken & people were trying to save her, though the edge of the crater kept crumbling every time anyone got close.

A neighbor saw Strawberry-Witch & Water-Witch & recognized them for what they were. "You! Witch-Gods! Help this girl!"

Water-Witch looked at her feet. Strawberry-Witch tried to explain. "We can't. We can barely do anything."

The other pot workers agreed. Water-Witch & Strawberry-Witch were some of the worst workers on the farm. "What are you good for, then? What is a god, anyway?" the neighbor asked.

BONE DEATH COUGHING SOUNDS

The little girl died. They couldn't get her out of the pit, & the edges kept crumbling. Water-Witch & Strawberry-Witch held hands & cried. The crater stayed a crater. Others began to emerge in the area as well. There was apparently a system of caverns beneath the whole region that decided now was the time to collapse. Everyone felt the instability. Strawberry-Witch & Water-Witch began sleeping in the same bed. They did holy things with their clits & asses & mouths & held each other with their arms & legs. They kept each other safe as much as they knew how. They did a ceremony for the little girl, which was really a ceremony mourning their inability to save her. They were not the kind of gods who could save her & this thought made them feel as unstable as the ground they walked on.

Strawberry-Witch eventually went back to where she had lived before. Water-Witch cried & hugged her & they made plans to meet again. Water-Witch continued to work at the farm for the next few weeks. During that time her evenings got strange. She was very, very lonely. The loneliness was a fist in her chest that wouldn't unclench.

Water-Witch stayed at the pot farm until they told her to leave, so she packed her things & drove to her sister's house. Her sister wasn't home. The door was unlocked in the back so she went inside. Where the living room couch usually would be there was a banana slug the size of the living room couch. Everything else was just as she remembered it. Don't leave me, the slug said, twitching. *I am so sorry*, said Water-Witch. *But I have to. I don't have anything at all.*

Water-Witch drove on to the coast. Reality got thicker. She realized she was trying to create any feeling inside of herself other than fear. She killed herself in her mind over and over. Why am I even here, she thought. This is all hurt. At the beach there were thorns that stuck in her tights. The whole planet spun slowly. It's not important or interesting. Death as a stopping place. She felt her tights rip. They were already covered in sand. The world is dying & nothing can help it, she thought. How am I a whole person. I can't do anything at all. I'm barely here as it is. There was sand in her mouth. When you squeeze any skin hard enough the sun comes out. It's my fault. What if it could be over in a way that's no big deal. It's not important. A stopping place. It started to rain/it got too cold/she walked to the car shivering. This isn't because of anything.

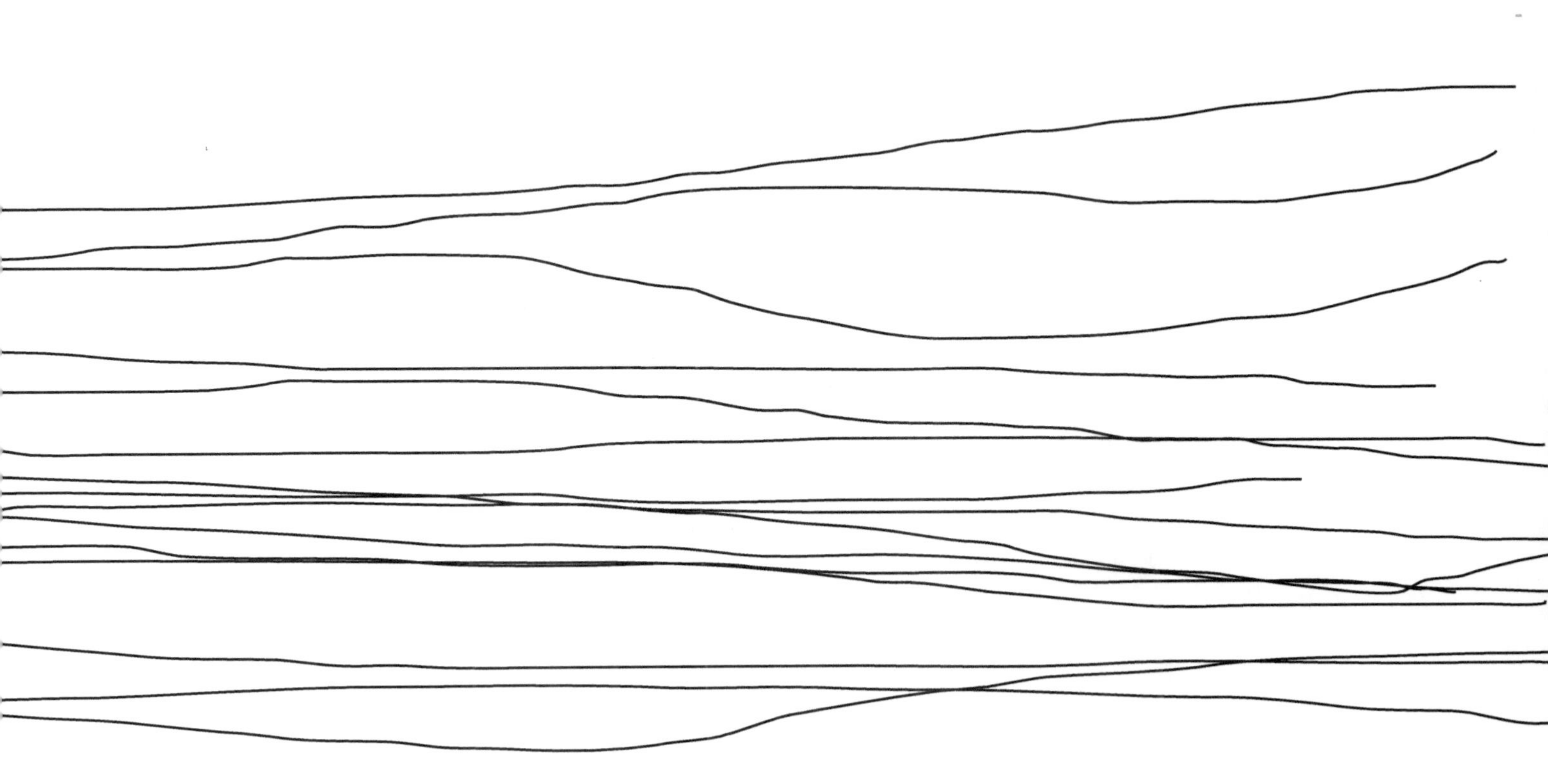

Water-Witch's least favorite thing about herself is that she keeps waking up. In all truth, mornings were the easiest time but after awhile it all slid into each other. Mornings slid into afternoons, slid into evenings, slid into times when everyone was sleeping & "cold" became an immersive physical/psychological experience. Water-Witch learned what to do to make time move slow or fast but never figured out how to make it go away. No matter how much time passed, there was always more of it. Water-Witch thought it was kind of fucked up, honestly.

Water-Witch decided to call Strawberry-Witch on the phone. Water-Witch cried to her. She said she missed her, & that things had been terrible. She told her about the bottomless feeling, the doom that wouldn't wash off. How it settled in after dark. How dark kept coming earlier as winter came. Strawberry-Witch was so sweet. She made plans to see Water-Witch again. They talked of doing things together & for a second Water-Witch thought she could be a person, but the phone call ended & Water-Witch found herself staring at her hands again, flexing her fingers, imagining her skull splitting on concrete.

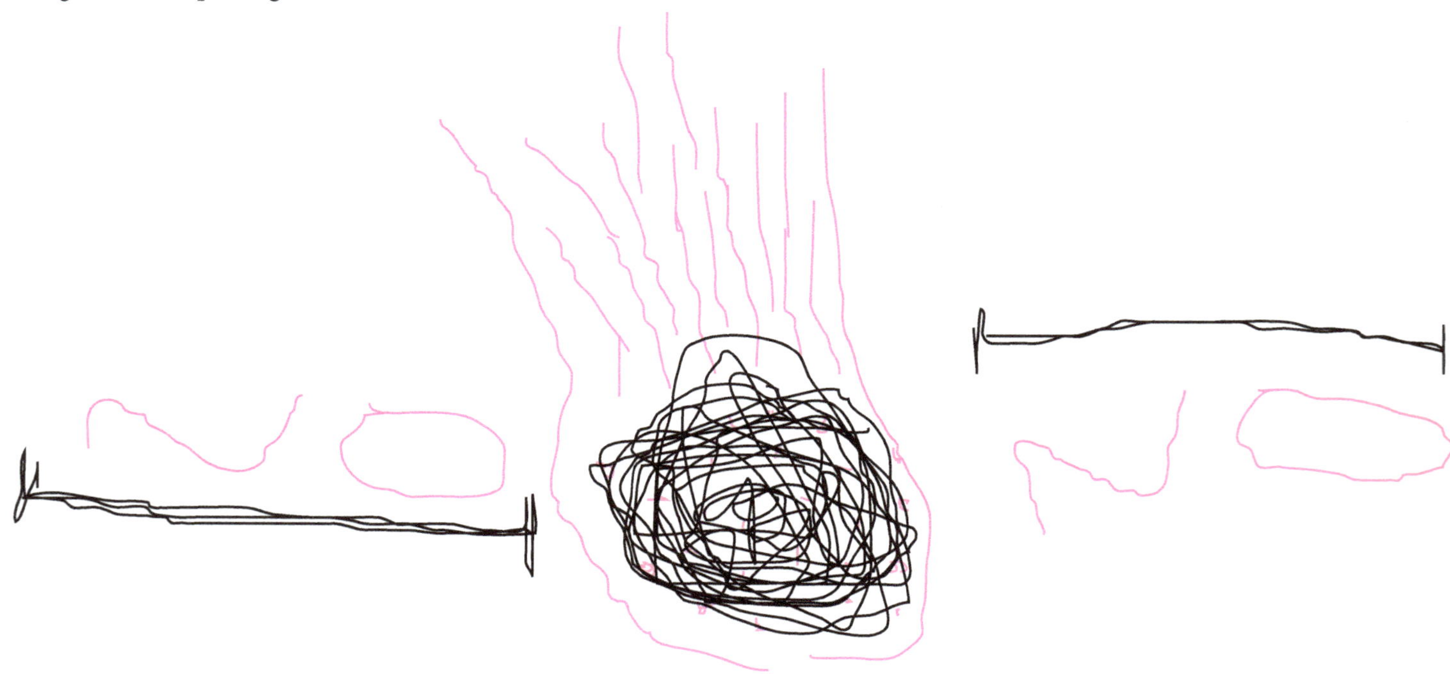

beginning

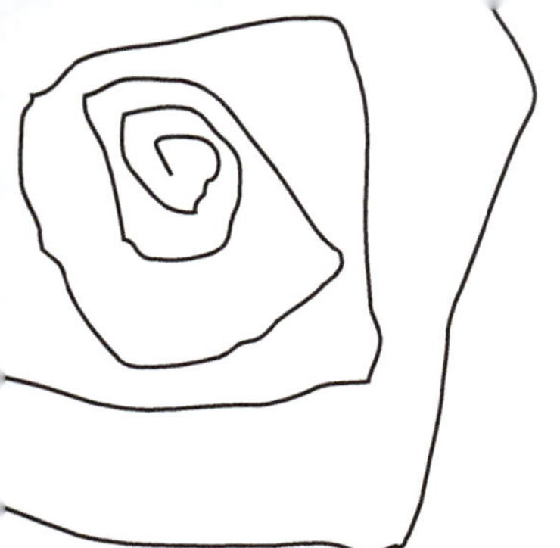

I AM AN ENEMY
I AM AN ALTAR

Feel The Wind,
Notice The Sky

A Rocky Stairway Winding Up And Around The Mountain
You Have Magick Powers
Look Into The Rays Of The Sun

- Nathaxnne Walker
from their review of the 1990 film
Games Children Play

LIFE
there is
nothing

I am so tired about Sea-Witch. I miss her dearly & want to hold her. At the same time I cannot assume that the disease that changed my brain & made me leave has gone. I want to help heal her. I want to heal myself.

I am living now inside the arms of a bright warmth that lets me live. She is like Sea-Witch in many ways. She might be Sea-Witch. When I was living in Sea-Witch reality was fluid, as was time. I am still in Sea-Witch & so I call this bright warmth "Sea-Witch" even though I have left her. Still I miss her and my time there. The following is a list of feelings I have had recently:

1. The feeling of being hunted.
2. The feeling of being the one hunting me.
3. A ball of cold metal inside my stomach that expands irregularly, points of which rupture some organs & just barely pierce my skin.
4. Standing on a beach while comforting someone in mourning.
5. Harm. Direct, ruthless harm.
6. A huge bird eating a building.
7. Being inside that building while it was eaten. Continuing what you were doing anyway.
8. A sweet animal putting its chin on my leg. Touching the animal. Feeling her fur.
9. Being completely naked in a room entirely full of soft cotton.
10. Last night I buried my head six inches deep in a wood floor.
11. Feeling the ache of that injury the next morning. Vomiting.

The bright warmth wants to go with me. She holds me in my fits. I hold her back. I still pray to meteor sometimes, but these days I find myself praying for thanks as much as for destruction. Whenever I pray like this Meteor prays back & tells me that it was not her doing. *My power is limited,* she prays. *I'm kind of a one trick pony.*

Moss-Witch knows the whole room around her is too big. Everything in it is too big. It's all too close to her face. Empty delivery food containers. A phone that is modern, new, but echos deeply some nearly forgotten piece of technology from her childhood. *What is it*, she thinks. She stares at the phone until it too becomes too close to her face and she has to look away. *My whole life has been like this*, she thinks. *Why does it still feel strange?*

Moss-Witch has to take a shit. She walks to where her body takes her for this and sits. The room zooms in and out arbitrarily. *This is so tired. I'm so tired of this*, she thinks. The word *landmarks* emerges in her brain and she tries to use it to create an escape, back into something she can feel confident about. But she abandons it when she thinks about other times she has been confident. Those times were embarrassing. She clears her mind and feels distinctly three feelings in quick succession: nostalgia, comfort, claustrophobia. She sticks it out for three more (fatigue, tingling and deep sadness) before she wipes, stands, flushes. *What the fuck*, she says out loud.

She closes her eyes & feels the sensation of other people being in the room. *Did I just shit in front of other people?* She panics briefly. Was that a chair or a toilet. She opens her eyes & checks. Toilet. Good. Safe. She exhales. The reactions of the people who aren't there echo in her mind. *I am an enemy.* I am an altar. *Don't forget me.* Never leave.

MORE THAN ANYTHING MONSTERS WANT TO BE ALLOWED TO LIVE & BE OKAY

"There is a sweetness here. Something I want to stay inside."

"I always want to stay inside."

"Not like that. I want to leave."

"Don't leave."

"Not like that. Not like that."

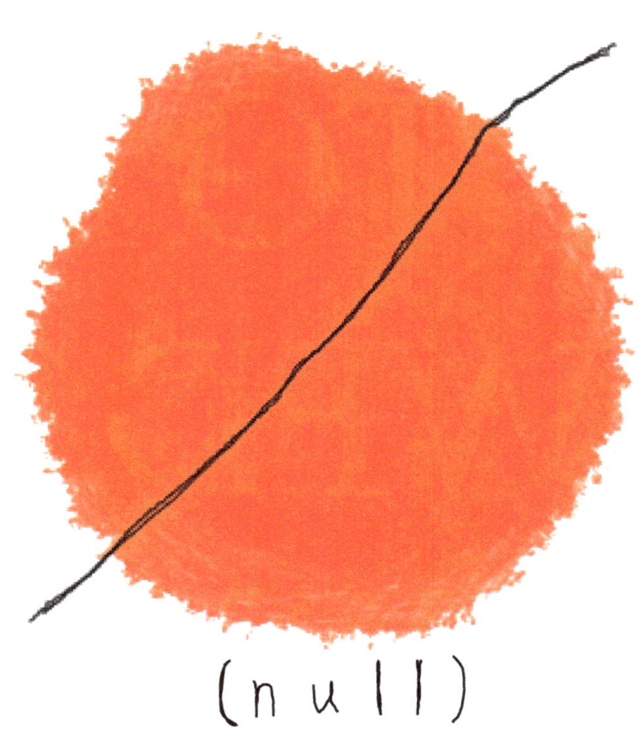

SEA-WITCH ANXIETY SPIT SQUARE TRIANGLE TRIANGLE

 In Sea-Witch everyone is tired. The monsters here sigh deeply & shrug their monster shoulders. We have heard tales that once we built monuments & discovered amazing things. That we once created beautiful, impossible works of art but these things have become damaged & lost across the centuries. Now living is done barely, & each day is spent attempting to get to the next. There is no sense of future, the past is painful to think of. We think of the long time they have ahead of them & despair. *Where is our culture*, we moan. *Where are the monsters we used to be, who could build, grow & thrive?* They are lost to us. We have not lost our love for each other, but it is always under threat as we have been hurt so often that we can no longer find the source. Today is a day, & soon it will end & be followed by another. We celebrate nothing. We organize nothing. We are nothing. What will become of us. May she lay us waste, we pray. May our ashes & bones fertilize the soil for lives better than ours. Lives that might be abundant with what we lack. With promise. With capability.

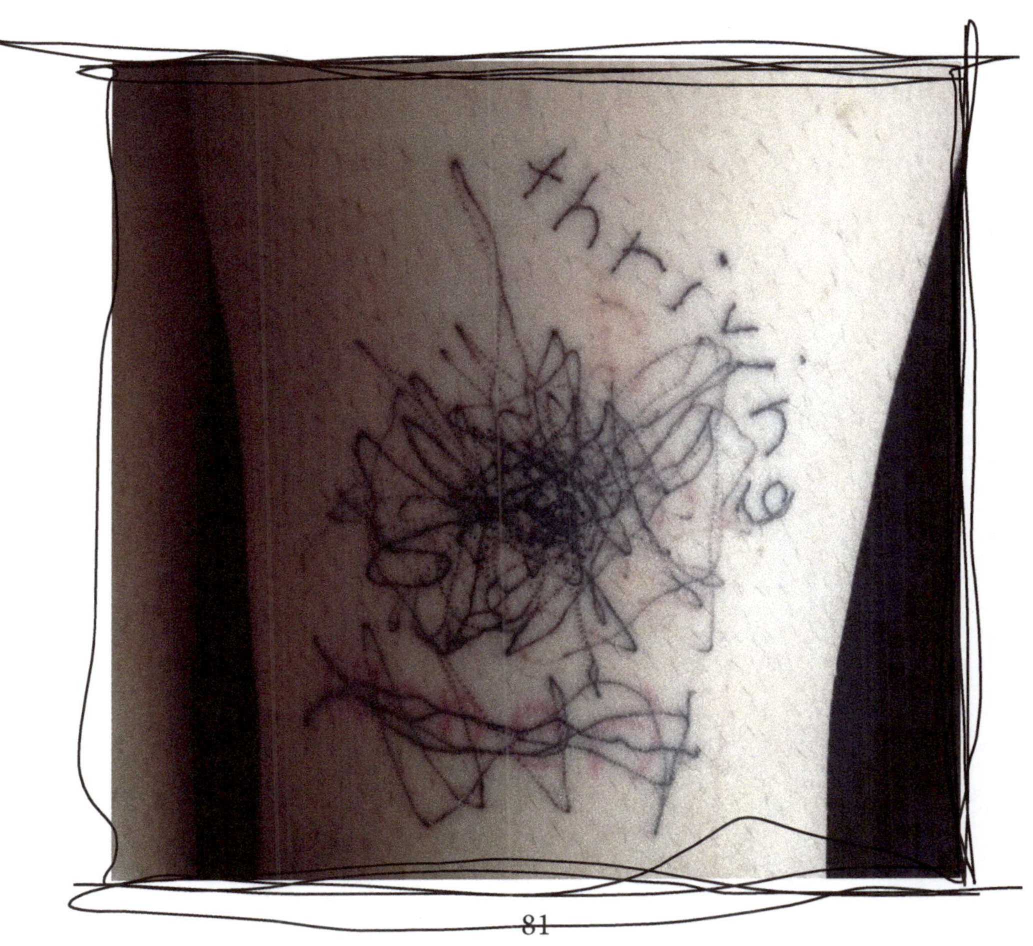

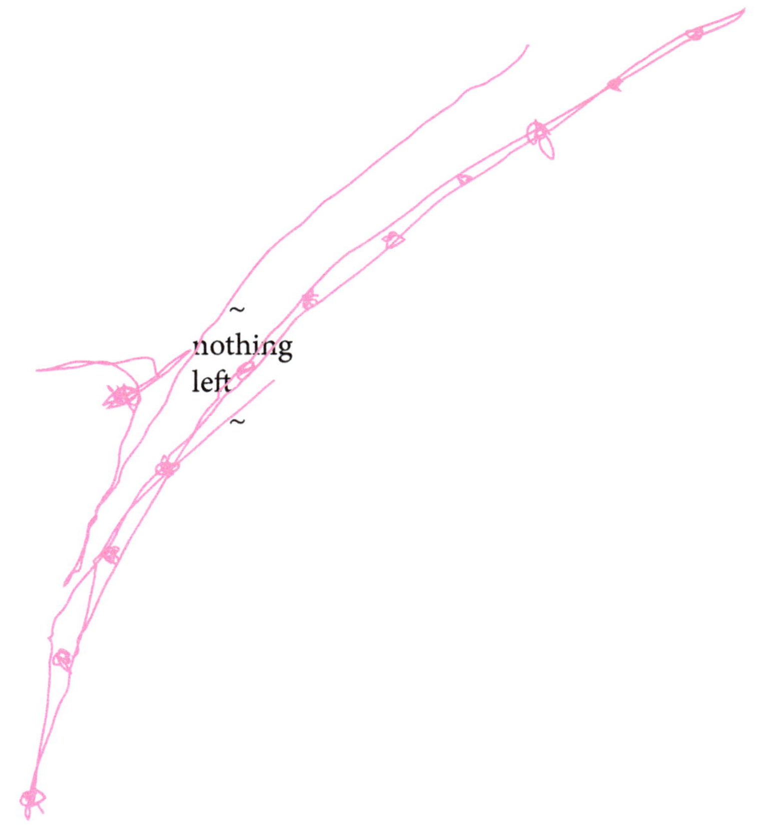
~
nothing
left
~

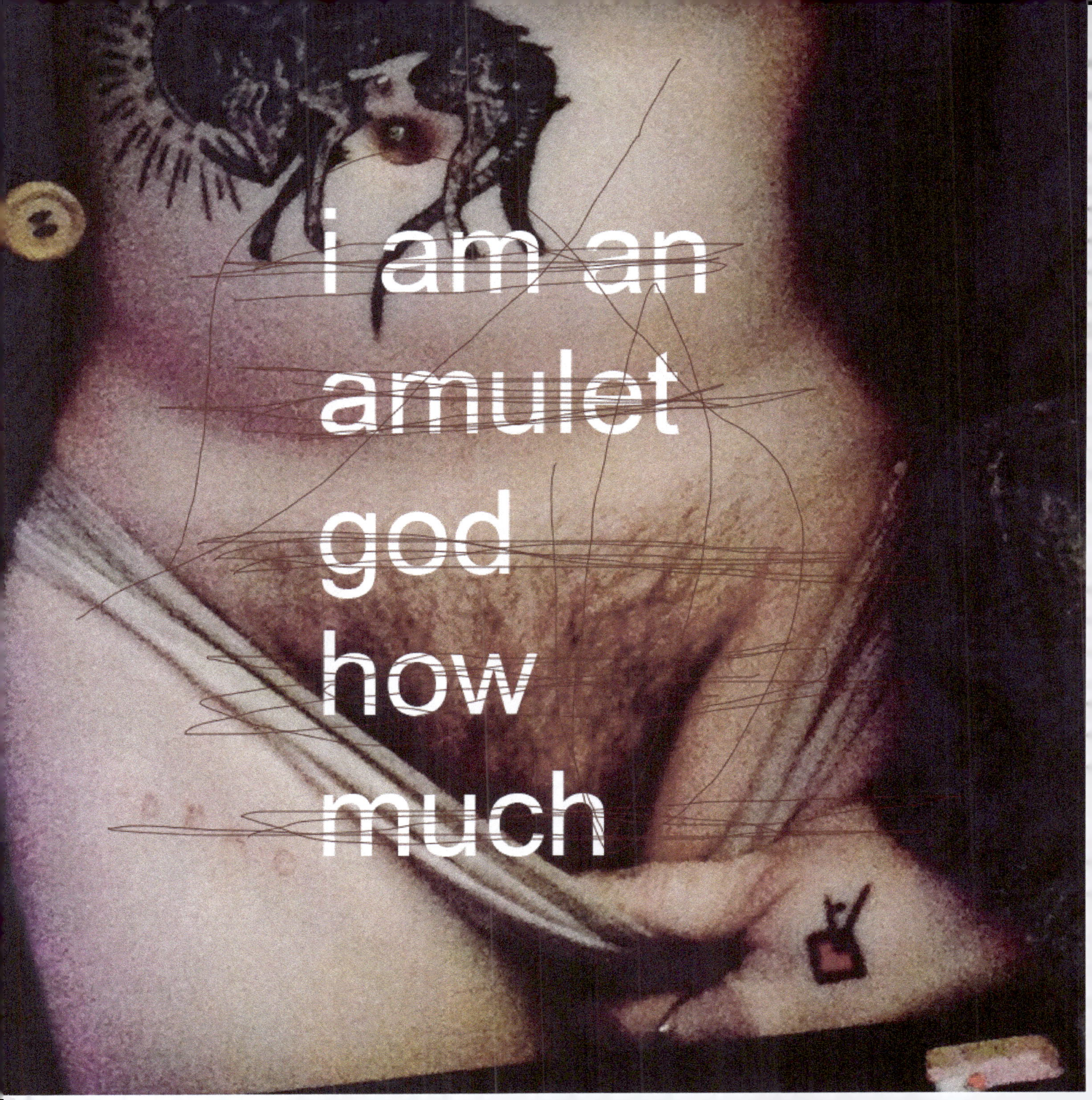

i am an
amulet
god
how
much

crimes
DIRT FUCK

Sit tight. There is going to be fire.

- Jordaan Mason, *The Skin Team*

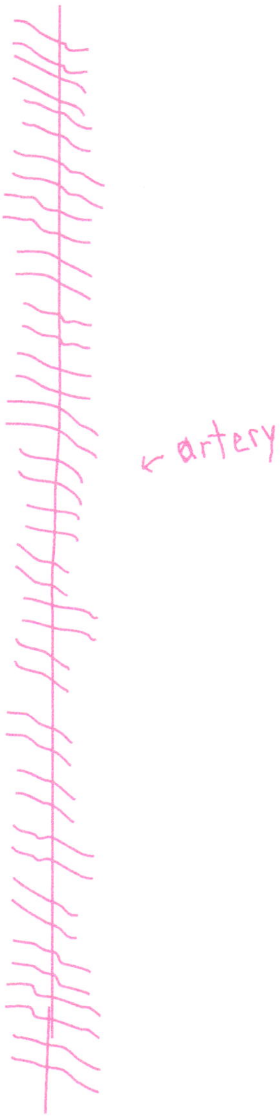

← artery

Dear Sea-Witch will we live in your body when u are dead/we will live in your body when u are dead..................................

....

....

....

....

....you are dead...

....

....

....

....

....

....

...........(how) does a witch-god die (there are so many dead witch-gods) when did they die (there are so many dead witch-gods) etc..

....

....

....

....

....

....

....

....

....

....the christmas of your body we live in...

....

....

....i am an enemy i am an altar where will we live when u are dead.................

....

....

....i am an enemy i am an altar do we still live in your body now that u are dead do we still live...

....

....................................do you still live in our bodies now that we are dead do you still live now that we are dead...........................

....i am an enemy i am an altar Dear Sea-Witch will we live (you   will   live)   will   u   live   (i   will   live)   when   is   it   over   i   am   an   ene-my..

....i am an altar no not even like..

....an altar will we still live inside u when u are here when we are gone do we still live inside u are an enemy u are an altar dead.............................

....
....fuck   time   altogether   i   am   an   altar...
....
....
....
....
....
....
.......i am six different gemstones of shining enemy my enemy our enemy i am so hot he tells me i am so hot ("how much just
2 lick") Dear Sea-Witch i am an altar lick will we still live in your body etc...
....
....
....
....
....how   much   fuCK   TIME   ALTOGETH-
ER...
....
....
....
....i   am   i   am   an   altar...
....
....i
am   an   enemy   i   left   sea-witch   when   i   was   living   in   sea-wit

ch...
....
....
....
...................................How much just to suck you off and eat your ass?..
....
....
....
....
....
....
....
....
....
....
....
....
....
....
....
....
....FUCK   OFF   I   AM   AN   ALTAR   I   AM   AN   ENEMYhow-
much)...
....
....
....
....
....

....
....
....
....
...............................Dear Sea-Witch, where will we live Dear Sea-Witch how much just to lick the altar...
....
....
....
....
....
....
....
....
....
....
....
....i am an altarpiece like family whats a family an enemy will we live in your dead
body (there are so many dead witch-gods)..
....
....
....
....
....
....
....i
am an altar fuck a family i am an altar how much to fuck me like an altar fuck me like an enemy (there are so many dead
witch-gods...
....
....
....
....
....

....
....
....
....
....
....) where will
u live when we are dead lets die at the same time lets die at the same fucking time may she lay us waste may she lay us may
we all get laid how much...
....
....
....
....
....
....
....
....
....to be an altar girlboy FUCK YOUR TIME ALTOGETHER THERE's too
much how much just to..
....
....
....
....
....
....
....
....
....be an enemy...etc......
....
....
....
....
....

....
....
....
....
....
....
....
....
....
....
....
....
....
....
....
....
....
....
....
....
....
....
....
....
....
....
....
....
....
....
....let go lets go Dear Sea-Witch where will we live
where will we live where will we live I AM AN ENEMY i am an altar i am an amulet god how much to fuck you in the ass
(there   are   so   many   dead   witch   -   gods)

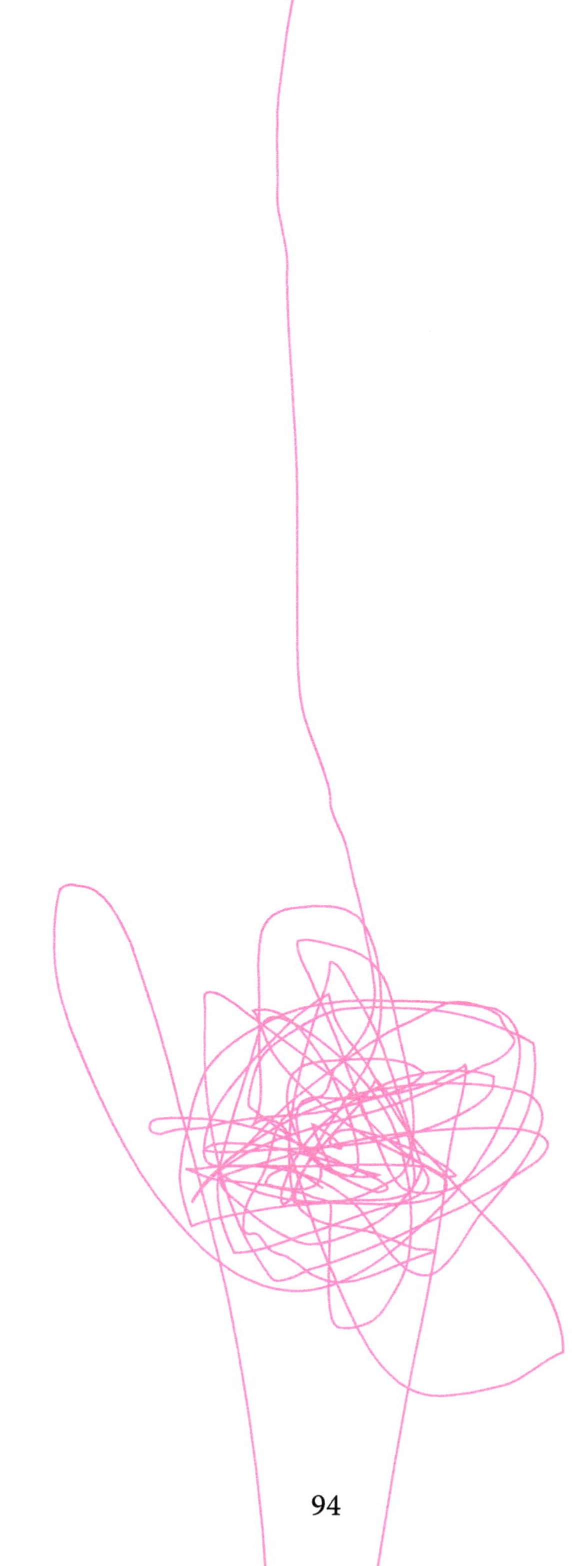

When they came for us, we didn't climb the trees. We thought about it, but there weren't any nearby consenting to be climbed. This was obviously an error in the calculations by our forebears. Let me start over. The 78 Men Who Cause Pain came for us. Of course they didn't come for us themselves, because they do nearly nothing themselves except that which causes their own pleasure at the expense of others, but they sent their cops in after us. I did not realize at the time that I was still living in Sea-Witch. I thought that the pain I had was great enough that surely I was outside of Sea-Witch, but I must have been wrong, because when the cops came in & began their bacterial destruction I found myself looking directly into the crying face of Sea-Witch, orange liquid pouring down her dark cheeks. She whispered *I'm sorry* & I whispered *thank you* before 8000 cops came & dragged us along the concrete until we were bloody. We yelled out things like *Fuck You* & *We Are Monsters* & *There Should Be Beaches Here I Thought There Were Beaches.* There were no beaches then though, only sound & concrete & flashes of red & blue bacterial light & concentrated pain that streamed from our heads down to the rest of us. The bacteria explained our "rights" to us. "Rights" are a thing made up by the 78 Men to describe the severely limited amount of movement one can make when tightly restrained. A scholar once explained that among people these "rights" are discussed as if they are freedom. As if they weren't present to remind us of all the things we are not allowed.

This is an ending of one kind. In this ending like all endings things can go on, even go on forever & no one will think of it as an ending at all. There are other endings as well, but for those whom this ending is for it is not an ending at all but an event that leads to others.

For example another ending is that as we were being slain & nearly slain by the cops we prayed for meteor (may she lay us waste) to come save us & she arrived in a peak of light in the sky that grew in flame-size to occlude all things. In this ending we die & so do the cops & so do the 78 Men & so do the living creatures & the witch gods & all restrained by time. In this ending not meteor (may she lay us waste) but Time is the killer & Time creates a new world from the ashes of this one, but we do not get to see it. In this ending everything dies.

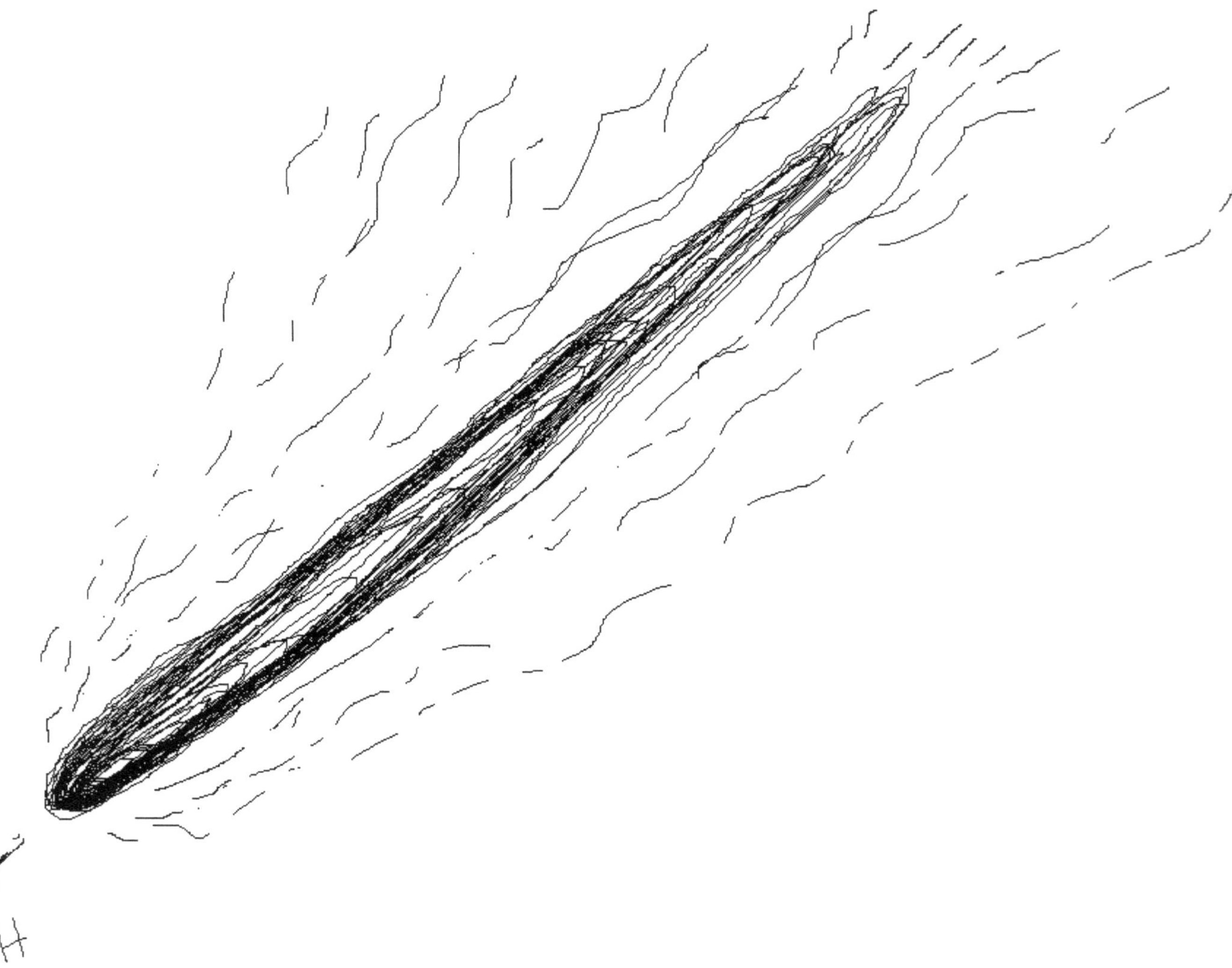

There are so many endings. In one the cops see us & realize they are not bacteria but monsters & they return to the 78 Men with us & we destroy them together against all odds. In this ending we create a world by & for monsters that encourages life & care beyond all else. In another ending the world is a rat having lunch & in this ending the rat eats the lunch (or does not eat the lunch & dies or skips lunch & eats dinner & is okay & says squeak squeak). In another ending light follows us in our paths & we glow much more brightly than before. In another ending I Am So Mad. In another ending nothing is real & this is the true ending. But because nothing is real truth is also not real & so this ending is only exactly as real as any other. In another ending I pull the suns from my body & the whole scene orbits them gently. In another ending I hate cops. Actually this is all endings. In another ending I am tired & fall asleep for awhile & dream of Sea-Witch & we explore each other's bodies with our bodies & she cums in my mouth & I cum in her mouth & we tell each other how good each other tastes. We awake in the trees, which consented & which we climbed when they came for us. We remember how the trees stretched up forever & how we arrived in the clouds where angels & living creatures surrounded us & fed us warm pierogies until we got better & were able to build again. Build again toward a place where we can live & expand our living to make space for the weakest above all, for they contain the magick for all life to finally begin. In this ending I change my name. In this ending I am a witch-god & realize I have always been so.

like a morning star
seam-ripping what
is left of night

may she lay us waste †

Questions:

1. Did I ever tell you how Dog-Witch died?

2. Did I tell you she died in the sea?

3. Did I tell you she made a promise to meteor (may she lay us waste) who in return made a promise back?

4. My neck is really sore.

5. Sea-Witch taught me about Dog-Witch, who formed her as a loving parent. Could you rub my neck?

6. That feels amazing.

7. Thank you.

8. A world was destroyed that is not ours & I feel like it is important for us to mourn that world. We know little about it but we do know that it was a place loved by many living things & many non-living things & that is enough for our mourning. Let me know if you have any questions for me. I'll be around for awhile. I'm always open to questions.

This is volume two of Sea-Witch. The text of this book and of volume one was origi-
nally published at the Sea-Witch patreon. You can subscribe to read the text of future
volumes of Sea-Witch before they are put into print at
http://patreon.com/monstr

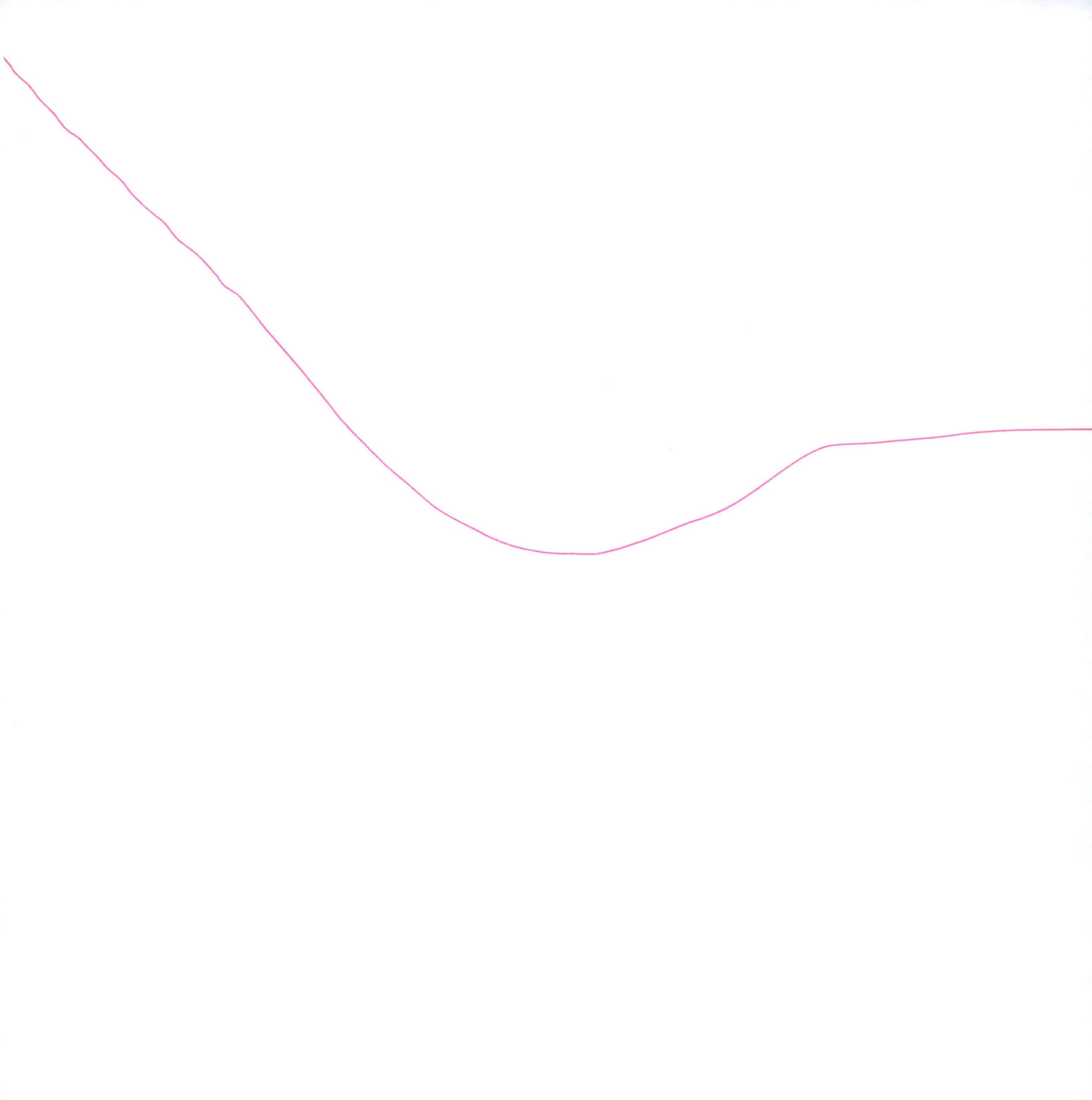

ABOUT THE AUTHOR

Moss Angel the Undying is a an angel sorceress living in Oregon. In a past book they listed they were a Scorpio sun/Taurus rising/Virgo moon & they would like to correct this grevious mistake. They are actually a Scorpio sun/Pisces rising/Virgo moon. Find them online at http://undying.club

THANKS

Thanks to my wife Døgtail for literally everything. You are beautiful & wild & I love you so much. Thanks to Jade of Spiders. Yr so connected and understanding & I love & appreciate you greatly. Thanks to Irene for teaching me so many of the ideas that were the basis for all of this work. Thanks to Opal and the other wonderful ppl at Watershed: Lilac, Peter, Remedy, Solo. This would have been so much more difficult to create without this beautiful healing space to do it in. Thanks to Delta & Skye & Clover for being rad & supportive, both of me & of Sea-Witch. Thanks to Joseph at 2fast2house for putting these books out. Yr the best editor ever. Thanks to The Wanderer crew for being so amazing and supportive: Colette, Raquel, Ginger, y'all are so fucking good. Thanks 2 El Pearson for being super supportive of Sea-Witch & being an amazing editor & person. As always thank you to all the beautiful monstrs who inspire this. I love you all. Let's burn this shit down & care for each other.

sigil of doing things, feeling good, & caring about people
by moss angel the undying

sigil of ending capitalism, healing trauma, and hot trans makeouts
by claire diane

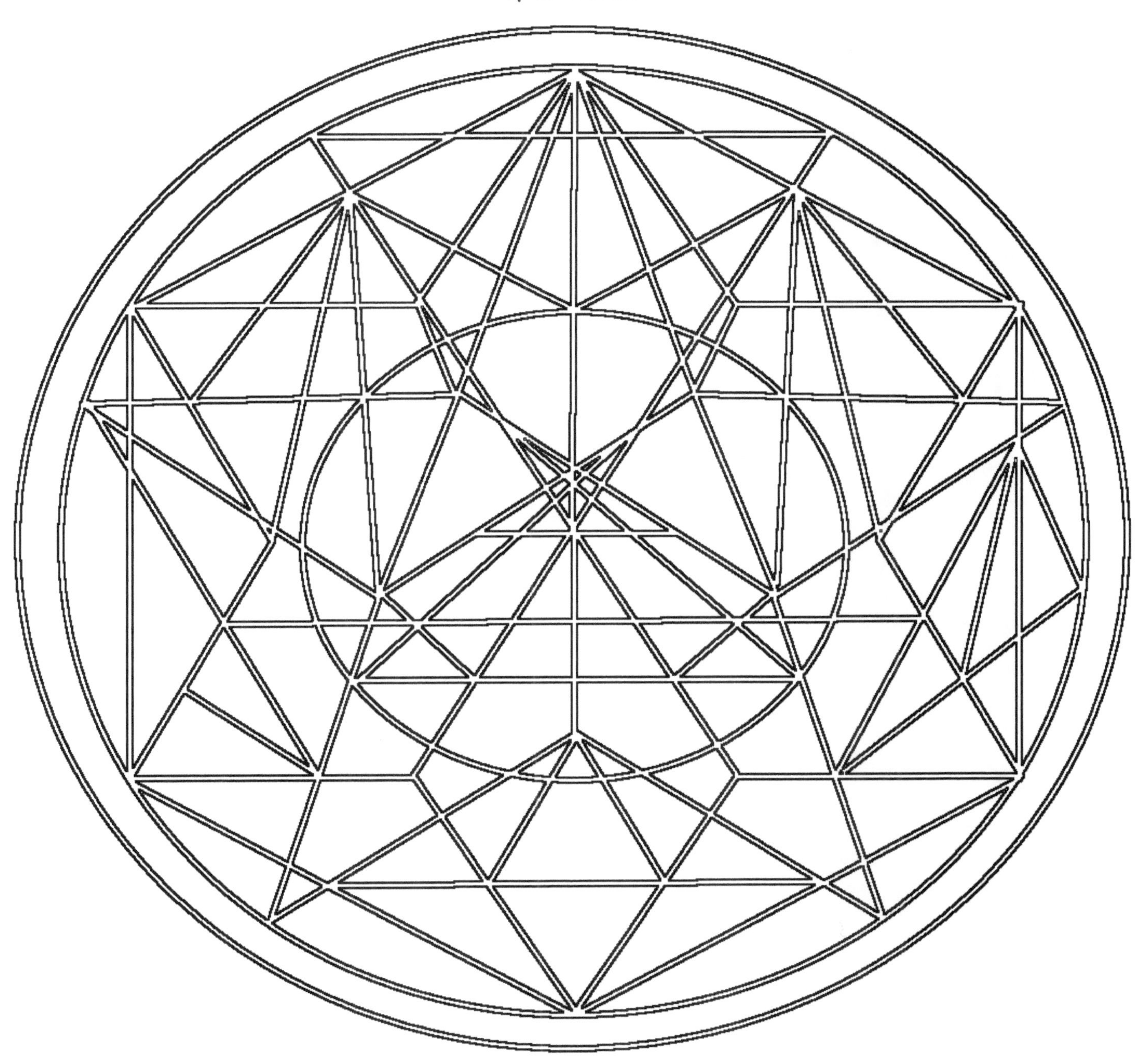